GREATEST
BATTLES

FOR BOYS

THE WAR ON TERROR

BY

RYAN RHODERICK

Greatest Battles for Boys: The War on Terror

Copyright © 2021 Ryan Rhoderick

All images are courtesy of the public domain unless otherwise noted.

Dedicated to the memory of all those who lost their lives on September 11, 2001.

CONTENTS

1. PRELUDE TO THE SEPTEMBER 11 ATTACKS

Figure 1. The World Trade Center (WTC)

The World Trade Center (WTC) was a massive complex of seven buildings in the Financial District of downtown Manhattan in New York City (Figure 1). Two of the complex's buildings, known as the Twin Towers, were the tallest buildings in the world from the day they were opened on April 4, 1973, up until Chicago's Sears Tower—currently Willis Tower—surpassed them in less than a year. They stood at around 1,365 feet each, accommodating 50,000 workers and 200,000 daily visitors.

During its existence, the WTC complex witnessed several incidents such as a fire that occurred on the 11th floor of the North Tower (1 WTC) on February 13, 1975, a bombing in the underground garage of 1 WTC on February 26, 1993, and a bank heist of $1.6 million at the Bank of America in 1 WTC on January 14, 1998. In 1998, the owner of the WTC complex, the Port Authority of New York and New Jersey, decided to privatize the WTC by leasing the buildings to a private company. The lease was awarded to Silverstein Properties in July 2001.

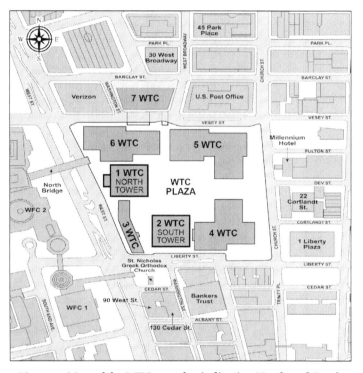

Figure 2. Map of the WTC complex indicating North and South Towers

YouTube

Building The World Trade Center 1970s Stock Footage by Buyout Footage Historic Film Archive:
https://www.youtube.com/watch?v=SMzEMFkW6i8

1.1 THE FIRST WTC ATTACK
FEBRUARY 26, 1993

Figure 3. The first WTC attack on February 26, 1993

In the early morning in New Jersey, across from New York City, a car followed a van filled with 500 kilograms of high-powered explosives. The man driving that van was Ramzi Yousef (Figure 6), a Pakistani man claiming refugee status in America. In the car behind him, following him on his errand, was his accomplice. On their way, Yousef realized he was dangerously close to running out of gas. He pulled off to a gas station to fill up his van. Police officers in a patrol car parked nearby took an interest in the car and van. Yousef tried to stall for time. He popped the hood of his van and pretended to have engine trouble. After a short while, the police lost interest and drove away. When they were out of sight, Yousef closed the hood, got back inside, and started moving his bomb-on-wheels towards his target, with his accomplice following close behind.

They crossed the bridge and drove into New York City. They headed towards the World Trade Center. Before noon, Yousef drove into the underground parking lot, just beneath the North Tower of the WTC. He parked his van by a support pillar.

Yousef climbed into the back of the van where his enormous bomb was. He used a lighter to light four 20-foot fuses. They caught on fire and shot sparks as the flame moved along the cord towards its final destination. The fuse was just long enough to give Yousef enough time to escape. Yousef then got into the second car, driven by his accomplice, and they made their exit, driving out the same way they came in.

Twelve minutes later, the burning fuses reached the explosives' blasting caps. That moment, at 12:17 pm, was the first Islamic terror attack in the United States of America.

The bomb rocked the building, but it was not nearly powerful enough to take down the tower. Despite that, six people died from the explosion, and over 1,000 people were injured.

Investigators got to work immediately. They easily traced the van back to a mosque in Brooklyn. There they found several suspects that could have been involved. Most of them were immigrants who were not associated with any terror group.

It wasn't long before the FBI concluded that Ramzi Yousef was the culprit and mastermind of the operation. Yousef sent a letter to the *New York Times* (*NYT*) saying the bombing was a retaliation against the US for their support of Israel and the oppression of the Palestinian people. Before the FBI could find him, Yousef had fled to Pakistan, where his trail went cold for nearly two years.

Figure 4. Damage caused by the first World Trade Center attack on February 26, 1993

Late 1994

Almost two years later, Yousef was in Manila, the capital of the Philippines. He was using an ordinary apartment as a bomb-making factory. He was developing a new plan to attack the US with a nitroglycerine-based explosive that could be hidden inside contact lens fluid cases. The bomb used nine-volt batteries as a detonator, small enough to hide inside a boot. For a timer, he used an ordinary Casio watch.

He had big plans for this bomb, but he decided he wanted to test his new weapon before using it against America. He chose an airplane at the Manila airport to be the subject of his violent experiment. He purchased plane tickets and easily snuck the tiny bomb on board. He armed the bomb and hid it in a pocket in his seat. When the plane landed, he got off. The bomb was still on the plane.

Soon after, that plane filled with new passengers and took off for its next destination: Japan. At 11:43 am, the plane was just passing near Osaka when the bomb detonated.

The bomb wasn't powerful enough to take the plane down. The airplane was rocked, but the pilots were able to make an emergency landing. Yousef's experiment killed one passenger and injured ten others. Investigators didn't understand why the attack happened or who did it.

Less than a month later, Yousef and a fellow bomb-maker accidentally started a fire in the worst possible place to start a fire: a bomb-making factory. The two men couldn't put the fire out and fled. After the fire department put the fire out, the police looked inside. They found fake priest costumes and pipe bombs. They planned to assassinate the Pope, who was coming to the Philippines in a few days to visit. Now, the police knew exactly who they were looking for. Yousef fled once again to Pakistan.

On Yousef's computer, police found his plan for tiny bombs. The plan was called "Codename: Bojinka." The plan was to bomb a dozen airline flights simultaneously, hoping to kill as many as 4,000 people. Luckily, that accidental fire put a stop to that plan. This was a complicated, experienced plan that required a lot of money. It was becoming clear that Yousef was not the mastermind of the WTC bombing. Someone else was helping him from the shadows.

Yousef escaped the police, but his accomplice was arrested. During the police questioning, the accomplice told them that he was a trained airplane pilot. He also admitted that there was a plan to crash small private planes filled with explosives into American landmarks and that he was recruited specifically because he could fly a plane. One of the targets was the Central Intelligence Agency (CIA) headquarters in Virginia (Figure 5).

Figure 5. CIA headquarters in Virginia

This information was then shared with the CIA. They immediately evaluated which landmarks they believed were most likely to be attacked, such as the White House, the Capitol, or Wall Street. That report was just six years before 9/11. Yousef was now the target of a worldwide manhunt. The US offered $2 million for information leading to Yousef's arrest. The bounty worked. Someone within his terror group in Pakistan gave him up for the reward money.

February 7, 1995

Yousef was arrested by Pakistani law enforcement and handed to the US. He was tried and sentenced to 240 years in prison. He gave one interview. In that interview, he told the journalist that he was a member of a new international terror network that was coming for America. The journalist knew a lot about foreign affairs and realized Yousef talked about the Islamic terror network called Al-Qaeda.

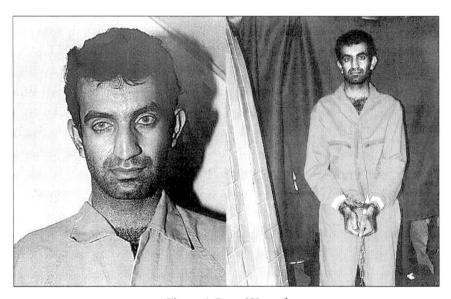

Figure 6. Ramzi Yousef

There was no doubt now. Yousef was not a terrorist mastermind. He was just one of many soldiers. They caught Yousef, but they didn't catch the people behind him.

While in prison, Yousef called his uncle Khalid Sheikh Mohammed (KSM) (Figure 7). In prison, all calls are

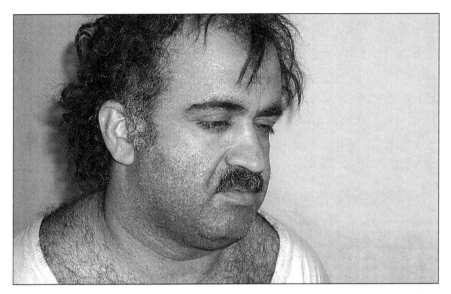

Figure 7. Khalid Sheikh Mohammed (KSM)

monitored and recorded. Because Yousef was part of a dangerous terror network, counter-terrorism police kept a close watch on everyone he spoke to and everything they said, just in case he made a mistake that could lead them to other terrorists. Yousef calling his uncle KSM gave law enforcement a reason to look at KSM. After investigating Yousef's uncle, they determined that KSM had put up the money for the first WTC attack.

KSM was far away, living in Qatar. The White House decided they should try to kidnap KSM and bring him back to America to try him for the crimes of financing terrorism and planning attacks against airplanes. The CIA said they couldn't do it. The military said they could, but the plan they offered looked more like a total invasion of Qatar than a kidnapping. President Bill Clinton (Figure 10) felt he didn't have any good options. The President reached out to the Emir of Qatar and asked directly for help apprehending KSM. An Emir is an Arabic word for a man who is a king or who is high-ranking in the military. KSM disappeared immediately after that phone call. Someone in the Qatari government tipped him off. KSM's name was added to the list of international terrorists. He was indicted of terrorism in absentia. That means he was found guilty automatically because he didn't appear in court.

KSM fled to Afghanistan. There he found another terror financier named Osama bin Laden (Figure 8).

Figure 8. Osama bin Laden

US intelligence was already interested in Osama bin Laden since the first WTC bombing in 1993. Bin Laden was a very wealthy man, and he was known to give money to terrorists to help them. He was also very easy to spot in a crowd because he was very skinny and very tall, and he always wore traditional white robes. Bin Laden was added to the list of suspects.

1996

Bin Laden was a significant player in the international terror group known as Al-Qaeda, which means "The Base." He was living in Afghanistan as the Taliban's guest—the Taliban was a religious dictatorship that ruled Afghanistan at that time.

While he was there, bin Laden was publicly calling for jihad against the United States. The word *jihad* has two different meanings in Islam. It can mean a spiritual struggle to spread or protect Islam. It can also mean a religious war. Bin Laden meant war. The CIA realized he was much more than a money man. He was a good organizer, charming, and very good at inspiring people to join his cause. In 1997, bin Laden opened a training camp. Mujahideen, soldiers who fight in holy wars, came to Afghanistan from all over the world to train in bin Laden's camps. There they learned tactics, weapons, and how to make bombs.

1998

Bin Laden wasn't making any effort to hide. He invited journalists to see his training camp (Figure 9) and gave interviews, allowing reporters to record videos of the training. Bin Laden even organized a press conference. At that conference, he announced that he was joining forces with the Egyptian group called Islamic Jihad. He called this merger the International Islamic Front for Jihad Against the US and

Israel. Al-Qaeda was joining together with this front. Bin Laden issued a 12-page declaration of war against the US publicly.

Mullah Mohammed Omar (Figure 9), the Taliban leader, allowed bin Laden to operate in Afghanistan. Still, he was concerned that bin Laden was becoming too powerful and was creating his own small army within Omar's country. Omar kept a close watch on bin Laden and gave him a mansion to live in so that he could always keep an eye on him.

Mullah Mohammed Omar

Al-Qaeda Training Camp

Figure 9. Mulla Mohammed Omar and Al-Qaeda Training Camp

The Taliban was keeping a close watch on bin Laden, and so were the Americans. The CIA was watching him at all times, using satellite photography and local spies to track his every move. They knew bin Laden was trouble and responsible for several acts of terror and murder.

The CIA began developing a plan to arrest bin Laden and bring him to the US for trial.

The CIA recruited a team of Afghan commandos to storm the mansion that bin Laden was living in and make the arrest. The raid was scheduled for June 23. Just before giving the green light, President Clinton had doubts. There was a debate at the White House. The President was getting cold feet and was concerned about the number of people who would die in this raid. This debate went on for a few weeks. Clinton was not yet convinced that bin Laden was worth risking other lives to capture. Al-Qaeda attacked America just two weeks after the scheduled date for the commando raid that never happened.

Figure 10. US President Bill Clinton in 1993

August 7, 1998

Al-Qaeda used truck bombs to destroy American embassies in the African cities of Dar es Salaam and Nairobi (Figure 11).

These attacks killed 224 people and injured 5,000 others. It wasn't long before US intelligence determined it was bin Laden's work. Clinton was no longer on the fence. He was ready to fight.

Figure 11. Destroyed US embassies in Dar es Salaam and Nairobi

August 20, 1998

CIA intelligence told the White House that bin Laden would be meeting with other high-ranking Al-Qaeda leaders at a training camp. Clinton decided they could hit all of the Al-Qaeda leadership in one blow if they fired a long-range cruise missile (Figure 12) into the meeting. They did just that, launching a missile that flew over the entire nation of Pakistan and into the meeting. A lot of Al-Qaeda leaders were killed, but not bin Laden. He wasn't killed because he wasn't there. Either the CIA had faulty intelligence, or bin Laden changed his plans at the last minute. In either case, with so much of the Al-Qaeda leadership dead, bin Laden was now one of the most important men in the organization.

The White House was not ready to quit. Clinton authorized the CIA to kidnap bin Laden. Now it would be more difficult. After the cruise missile attack, bin Laden knew that the Americans were gunning for him. He became a lot more cautious than he had been. The CIA was always one step behind him. Bin Laden knew the CIA, and he knew how to evade capture. After all, the CIA taught him how in the 1980s. But that's a story for later on in the book.

Figure 12. Launch of a Tomahawk cruise missile

The CIA got a tip that bin Laden would be at the governor's mansion in Kandahar. American ships prepared to launch missiles at the mansion. The military was skeptical of the intelligence and warned that a cruise missile strike could kill

200 or more people. Not all of those people were terrorists. They could be innocent women and children. The attack was canceled, deeming the cost of civilian deaths to be too high. The governor's home was also very close to a mosque. The President was concerned that if they accidentally damaged the mosque with the missile, it would offend Muslims and create new enemies.

1999

The CIA gets a new tip that bin Laden will be hanging out at a falcon hunting camp in Afghanistan. Falcon hunting is a very popular sport for wealthy people in that part of the world, a lot like a country club. CIA operatives determined bin Laden would be staying at the camp for a few days. However, satellite photography also caught a glimpse of a C130 aircraft parked nearby, registered to the nation of the United Arab Emirates (UAE). This could only mean that important, high-level government officials from the UAE were also at the camp. The UAE was a good ally to the United States. Clinton did not want to risk killing members of an ally's government and creating an international incident.

They'd already failed to kill bin Laden once. They didn't want to keep missing. If the US tried and failed over and over again, it could make bin Laden look unkillable and make the US look weak, which would be a great recruitment tool for Al-Qaeda. That would be the last chance the US had to take down bin Laden. They didn't take the shot, and they would regret it.

January 2001

Bill Clinton handed off the presidency to George W. Bush. They met together, as outgoing and incoming presidents always do. In that meeting, Clinton warned Bush about bin Laden. He told Bush that he considered Al-Qaeda to be the biggest threat to the US and expressed that not killing bin Laden was his biggest regret.

Figure 13. US President George W. Bush in 2003

George W. Bush (Figure 13) was sworn in as the new President. Only five days later, the new President got a memo from his national security advisor that Al-Qaeda is a major threat and needs to be a priority. President Bush didn't take bin Laden's threats seriously.

Meanwhile, in Afghanistan, bin Laden was making preparations for the largest terror attack in human history.

YouTube

Sights, sounds of 1993 World Trade Center bombing by Eyewitness News ABC7NY:

    https://www.youtube.com/watch?v=VqQu2oD3-dU

The 1998 US Embassy Bomb in Dar es Salaam, Tanzania by AP Archive:

    https://www.youtube.com/watch?v=sCwlZPqaSJE

1.2 AL-QAEDA BEGINS PLANNING

KSM was the mastermind of the entire plan. After his nephew Yousef was arrested, he changed the original plan. KSM decided that small planes loaded with explosives wouldn't be very effective. He wanted to take down large buildings because they were easier to hit and sent a more symbolically powerful message. The new plan was to hijack large airplanes, like 747s (Figure 14), and crash them into buildings. They didn't know which buildings yet.

Figure 14. Boeing 747

Al-Qaeda had two operatives in mind for this mission: Khalid Al-Mihdhar and Nawaf Al-Hazmi (Figure 15). They were both from Saudi Arabia, which was a US ally. They both had US visas, and they were not known to authorities. Before going to the US, the two men got basic training.

KSM had them play flight simulators, which are like very realistic video games, to help them understand the basics of flying an aircraft. In the game, the two men crashed planes into buildings over and over again. KSM taught them techniques for hijacking planes, sometimes showing them Hollywood movies for example.

Figure 15. Khalid Al-Mihdhar and Nawaf Al-Hazmi

What KSM didn't know was that these men were already known to the CIA. Agents had been tracking them for two years. The National Security Agency (NSA) became aware of them when they were spying on a phone they knew had been previously used by Osama bin Laden. The CIA followed them to Malaysia, where they were photographed in a meeting with other Al-Qaeda members. A week later, they were sent to the US. They hopped on the plane, flew to the US, landed, and walked right through security with no problems. Something had gone wrong.

The CIA knew that Al-Mihdhar was a terrorist, but they didn't share that info with US immigration or the FBI. The CIA didn't put his name on a suspected terror list. The two terrorists should have been easily noticed and apprehended as soon as they landed in America.

This marks one of the biggest failures of US intelligence and security. At the time, different agencies were not good at sharing info. The FBI had information. The CIA had information. The NSA had information. If they had pooled all that knowledge together, they might have stopped what would be soon to come.

Now in the US, the two men went to a local flight school to take lessons. They were so bad at flying that the flight instructor told them it was a waste of their time and money to keep trying. They said they wanted to fly Boeings. The instructor said to them that it would be impossible if they couldn't even fly a small plane. The terrorists reported back to KSM that flying was harder than they thought it would be. Al-Qaeda needed qualified pilots who would have strong English-speaking skills.

2000

Back in Afghanistan, a new technology became available to the US that is now infamous: the predator drone (Figure 16). This was an unmanned surveillance aircraft, controlled remotely. On the very first mission with a drone, they flew it over bin Laden's home in Afghanistan. They saw a tall man in white surrounded by commandos in black. A few days later, they caught another video of the tall man in white. The CIA was sure the tall man was bin Laden.

Figure 16. Surveillance Predator drone and operators

At that time, predator drones were not weaponized. They could see bin Laden with the drone, but they couldn't attack. The CIA got started working on arming the drones with hellfire missiles immediately, but this process is a lot more complicated than they expected, and it would be a while before drones became the missile delivery systems that they are now famous for.

Bin Laden personally trained what they called "muscle hijackers," the guys who would intimidate passengers and get control of the planes. At this point, they were not told what the mission was besides hijacking a plane. They did not know that they were training to kill themselves in a suicide attack.

Once trained, the terrorists started traveling to the US. The total number was 19, including the two that were already in America. Just as the first two terrorists to come to the US should have been noticed and arrested the moment they landed, so did all but three of the 17 new arrivals. In total, 16 of the 19 Al-Qaeda operatives shouldn't have been let in. Only three were clean enough to get through the border. They should have been on a terrorist watch list, or they should have been denied because they had incomplete documents. They had bad visas or bad passports but were let in anyway. Had they stopped them there, the attack might never have happened.

Spring and Summer 2001

US intelligence got word that bin Laden has been looking to recruit trained commercial pilots as terrorists. Between that and what Yousef told them, they started to get a picture of what Al-Qaeda was planning.

June 22: The Federal Aviation Administration (FAA) got warned about potential attacks, and they warned all pilots of potential hijacking plots by Islamic terrorists.

June 25: Airlines were given a threat advisory that there was a high probability of an attack by Al-Qaeda.

August 6: President Bush got a daily brief in the morning, which was a document summarizing all the important things he needed to know that day. The brief was titled, "Bin Laden Determined to Strike in the US." The briefing connected bin

Laden and Al-Qaeda to Yousef, the first WTC bomber who used a van full of explosives. The briefing also clearly warned of potential airline hijackings.

August 2001: The CIA lost track of Al-Mihdhar and Al-Hazmi. It is illegal for the CIA to operate within the US, so they reached out to the Federal Bureau of Investigation (FBI) for help. This was the first time that the FBI was told about any Al-Qaeda terrorists inside the US. The CIA asked for the FBI's help in tracking them down, concerned that they may be attacking soon. Through the complex administrative process, the request was flagged as "routine." This gave the FBI a 30-day window for investigators to find the men.

September 10, 2001: The CIA reached out to the FBI office in Los Angeles and asked again for help finding the two known Al-Qaeda operatives.

September 11, 2001: All of the 19 hijackers boarded their planes in the morning. Every one of them knew the whole plan. They knew their targets. They were ready to die and kill thousands. It was too late now for the FBI or CIA to stop it. The attack was already underway.

YouTube

The Rise & Fall Of The Boeing 747 Jumbo Jet by Long Haul by Simple Flying:

   https://www.youtube.com/watch?v=g2iKZsYi_PY

MQ-9 Reaper UAV: The Most Feared USAF Drone in the World by US Military Power:

https://www.youtube.com/watch?v=EizQ4y39B1A

Movies

The Siege (1998)

This action thriller movie was made before 9/11, and it is spooky at how well it predicts the Al-Qaeda attacks that happened three years after it was made. It is a fictional account about a massive terror plot in New York by jihadi terrorists and the city's lockdown as the military declares martial law.

Directed by: Edward Zwick

Starring: Denzel Washington, Annette Bening, Bruce Willis, Tony Shalhoub, Sami Bouajila, and David Proval

Path to Paradise: The Untold Story of the World Trade Center Bombing (1997)

A drama history movie of the events leading up to the bombing of the WTC in New York in 1993 and the arrest of the terrorists. The FBI had a spy among the terrorists, but declined to pay him $500/week for more information. A story of incompetence on all sides.

Directed by: Leslie Libman and Larry Williams

Starring: Peter Gallagher and Marcia Gay Harden

2. THE SEPTEMBER 11 ATTACKS

You can measure time in minutes, hours, days, and years. In human experience, we measure time by experiences. There was a time before you could walk. There was a time after you learned to walk. There was a time you were in second grade and a time after. There was a time before your family moved and a time after. The exact number of minutes isn't important. Our memories aren't perfect clocks. We remember things as events, not dates on a calendar.

The attacks on September 11, 2001, usually called 9/11, were one such event. There was a time before 9/11 and a time after 9/11. We each have our own before and after moments, like walking and second grade. But 9/11 was a before-and-after moment that everyone shared.

Go ask anyone who is old enough to remember. Ask anyone older than 30 about what they were doing on 9/11. Every single person you ask will remember. They will remember exactly where they were, who they were with, what happened that day, and what they were feeling. Go ask them. They'll be happy to tell you.

Then ask them what they had for dinner four days ago. They probably won't remember. They don't remember something from four days ago, but they remember something from decades ago.

That's how important 9/11 is to America particularly, but also people all over the world.

2.1 A DAY THAT CHANGED EVERYTHING

Figure 17. September 11 attacks on the WTC, 2001

It was a clear day in New York. That morning, thousands of people started their morning commute to get to their job inside the WTC.

In Boston, American Airlines Flight 11 left Logan Airport at 7:59 am. Onboard were 92 people. Five of them were Al-Qaeda terrorists, intending to kill everyone aboard the plane, including themselves.

United Airlines Flight 175 left the same airport soon after. There were 65 people aboard. Five of them were Al-Qaeda terrorists.

8:14 am, Flight 11 is up in the air. Al-Qaeda hijackers take control of the planes. They are carrying box cutters. They get control of the passengers, claiming that they have a bomb and that they'll blow the plane up if the passengers try to resist. That's a lie.

In 2001, no one had ever attempted what these terrorists had planned. Terrorists hijacking planes was not new or uncommon. Terrorists took planes several times in the 1970s and 80s. They always took hostages. However, those terrorists just took hostages and made demands like any other kidnapping. They demanded money or the release of prisoners. These frequently ended without any bloodshed. Most people aboard the plane knew this. They believed that if they played it cool and didn't interfere, this would all be over soon, and they would probably be fine. The passengers just let the hijacking happen because they had no idea about the terrorists' real mission.

8:19 am, a flight attendant aboard Flight 11 called ground control and told them that the plane had been taken.

There are protocols in place for airplane hijackings. There are steps and procedures. They all failed on 9/11. The military would not be told about the hijacking for 18 minutes after the flight attendant told the ground. In the event of a plane hijacking, the military is supposed to be alerted immediately.

Nobody told the flight traffic controllers, either. They learned about the hijackings when they heard the hijacker's voice on the radio.

8:27 am, Flight 11 made a sharp turn off its planned course. The new pilot, a terrorist, Mohamed Atta, turned the plane towards New York.

Ten minutes later, Boston finally contacted the military to inform them of the situation. Out of sheer bad luck, the nearest airbase for the region was in the middle of a training exercise.

When they were told the news, they weren't immediately sure if this was part of the exercise or not. They had to be told several times, "No, this isn't an exercise."

The base went on alert and began to scramble to a pair of F-16s (Figure 19) to intercept Flight 11.

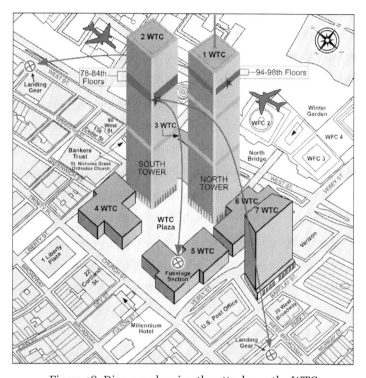

Figure 18. Diagram showing the attacks on the WTC

While those jet fighters were prepping, the hijackers aboard Flight 175 made their move. They took control of the plane and also changed direction towards New York.

8:46 am, Flight 11 from Boston arrived over New York City. With 92 people aboard, the Al-Qaeda pilot struck the North Tower at 470 mph (Figure 18). The impact created a massive explosion as the jet fuel caught on fire. The plane was moving so fast that it was nearly vaporized by the impact. Everyone on board was killed instantly, as well as everyone on the floors hit by the plane. Debris rained down onto the streets below. Everyone nearby was in a state of shock as they saw the most well-known and iconic buildings in the world explode. Throughout the entire city, the explosion could be heard. Countless people walked to the nearest window and looked out to see the tower on fire, smoke billowing out of it.

Figure 19. F-16

There was an immediate citywide emergency response. Firefighters, police, and emergency medical personnel all rushed towards the WTC. As they drove through the city, they passed by people on the streets and looked out of their windows, silently staring, speechless at the horror that they couldn't believe they were seeing. The F-16 fighters from Otis Airforce Base were not in the air yet.

They didn't get off the ground for seven more minutes after the first plane hit the WTC. When they were in the air, they flew towards New York at top speed, full afterburner the whole way. Their flight to New York took 32 more minutes.

8:55 am, New York traffic control realized a second plane had been hijacked. They reached out to the National Command Center (NCC) for help, but NCC told them they were already busy with the first hijacking. The military was not informed immediately.

New York traffic control was tracking United Flight 175. They watched on radar as it dropped in altitude and started circling New York.

9:03 am, Flight 175, with 65 passengers, crashed into the corner of the South Tower at 595 mph. The 78th-84th floors were destroyed in an incredible big explosion. The building looked like it had a big cut in it. This was all captured live on television. While the news was showing the damage to the North Tower from the first attack, the second plane crashed into the other tower. Millions were gathered around their TVs watching this at the very moment it happened.

The military didn't learn about the second hijacking until the moment it crashed into the South Tower. The jet fighters flying towards New York still hadn't arrived.

During these attacks, President Bush was at an elementary school reading to children.

9:05 am, Bush's chief of staff tells him the second plane has hit the other tower. He leaned to the President and whispered in his ear, "The United States is under attack."

For seven minutes, the President sat with the children before standing up and leaving. He later said he was trying to compose himself to project calmness to others.

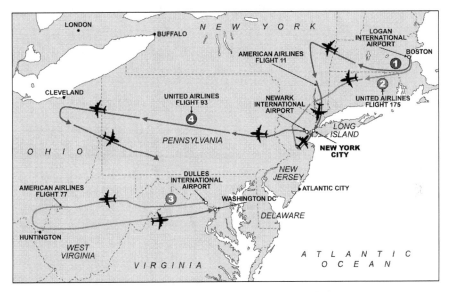

Figure 20. Flight paths of the four hijacked planes

Around the same time, American Airlines realized that another one of their planes, Flight 77, was hijacked. Flight 77 was heading for their unknown target in Washington DC (Figure 20), the capital of the United States of America. Getting this information to the military took a half hour.

9:23 am, all planes in the sky were warned that terrorists were hijacking planes and crashing them into buildings. All pilots were told to secure their cockpits. The pilot of United Flight 93 didn't understand and requested that control repeat themselves. Two minutes later, the cockpit was taken, and the hijackers were heard over the radio. The pilot didn't secure the cockpit.

Like Flight 77, United Airlines Flight 93 turned towards Washington DC.

9:30 am, President Bush made his first televised statement from Emma E. Booker Elementary School in Sarasota, Florida (Figure 21). The secure phone lines were all down, clogged by the unprecedented traffic within the federal government. Even on a private cell phone, the phones were clogged up, with everyone making calls at the same time all over the world.

President Bush At Emma E. Booker Elementary School

Air Force One

Figure 21. President Bush at Emma E. Booker Elementary School and Air Force One

During a national emergency of that kind, the procedure was to get the President onto Air Force One (Figure 21) and get into the air as soon as possible. The sky was the safest place for the President to be. However, phone communications were down. Air Force One was supposed to be used as the command center of America during an emergency, but the command center couldn't communicate with anyone.

People on the ground were terrified. They couldn't contact the President. They had no idea where he was, what his orders were, or if he was safe.

At the same time, a US Air Force cargo plane was already in the air looking for Flight 77. It almost collided with Flight 77, which was banking sharply. The cargo plane received a radio message from the ground to follow Flight 77.

The Pentagon **Before** The September 11 Attacks

The Pentagon **After** The September 11 Attacks

Figure 22. The Pentagon before and after the September 11 attacks

9:37 am, Flight 77 was piloted by Hani Hanjour. He was chosen because the Pentagon (Figure 22) was the hardest target to hit, and he was the best pilot Al-Qaeda had, with an FAA flying certificate. He dove low and crashed the plane and 64 passengers into the Pentagon, the headquarters of the US Department of Defense, the nerve center of the entire US military. Another 125 people inside the Pentagon were killed.

The White House was evacuated. Senior government officials were rushed off to secret locations and bunkers for their protection. America was in a state of chaos.

Figure 23. Air traffic controllers

9:42 am, the senior air traffic controller (Figure 23) ordered all planes in the air to land immediately. This was a very risky order, but they believed they needed to do something, anything, to get planes out of the sky.

At this time, there was still one more plane in the air with Al-Qaeda terrorists aboard: United Flight 93.

9:59 am, the fires in the towers were so intense that some people jumped out of the windows to their death to evade being burned alive. People trapped inside were calling for help or calling loved ones. Firefighters, police, and emergency rescue workers had been at the towers for almost an hour trying to rescue as many people from the building as possible. The South Tower had sustained too much structural damage. It began to bend and break apart. At 1,365 ft tall, and with 110 floors, countless tons of material crumbled and fell and shook the earth. The city was swallowed up by a cloud of smoke and dust. The sky turned tan. People were covered in ash from head to toe (Figure 24). No one could see more than a few feet in front of them. Victims staggered through the streets, dazed and wide-eyed. People panicked and escaped.

Figure 24. Emergency rescue workers and people covered in ash

10:03 am, United Flight 93 never made it to its target in DC. The plane crashed in a field in Pennsylvania. Passengers aboard the plane were able to learn that this was not a hostage hijacking. They knew that this plane was coming down no matter what, and they decided that if they had to die, they needed to stop the terrorists from using the plane to kill anyone else. The passengers fought the terrorists, and the Al-Qaeda pilot crashed it before letting it be retaken. The heroic actions of those passengers saved the lives of everyone that plane was targeting.

The military only learned that Flight 93 had been hijacked after it had crashed.

10:28 am, the North Tower of the WTC buckled and fell straight down. Thousands were dead. All electricity was shut down in Manhattan. No one could make phone calls. All the lines were jammed with countless other callers.

Figure 25. People fled the city either by walking or using boats

The collapse of the second tower struck the smaller nearby buildings, causing damage and starting fires in WTC buildings 4, 5, 6, and 7.

Building 7 was designated as the city's command center. It burned unchecked for seven hours.

5:20 pm, Building 7 collapses.

People began fleeing the city (Figure 25). The roads were not able to be driven on. Millions of people walked through Manhattan and across the bridges. Others escaped by using boats deployed by the Army Corps of Engineers.

A DAY THAT CHANGED EVERYTHING   39

In total, 2,977 civilians were killed, not counting the 19 hijackers themselves. There were 25,000 people injured. At least 200 firefighters died trying to rescue people in the buildings while they burned and finally collapsed.

Emergency responders worked nonstop tirelessly, digging through the debris with sniffing dogs, looking for any survivors. They found a few fortunate people and rescued them. Mostly they found bodies.

YouTube

9/11: Second plane hits South Tower by CNN:
   https://www.youtube.com/watch?v=sBciZFE8lAw

When the Towers Fell by National Geographic:
   https://www.youtube.com/watch?v=ieIFtjnBfJU

9/11: Survivors' Stories From That Day | I Was There by LADbible TV:
   https://www.youtube.com/watch?v=o76J9KwR_DM

Cameraman caught in aftermath of Twin Towers collapse on 9/11 by Eyewitness News ABC7NY:
   https://www.youtube.com/watch?v=OQk5Qw8hHGA

2.2 WHY WAS AMERICA ATTACKED?

The common phrase we heard after the 9/11 attacks was, "They hate us for our freedom." People indeed enjoy liberties in the West that some religious fanatics disapprove of. However, that was not the only reason.

Osama bin Laden explained precisely why he was attacking America by making a video of himself clearly stating his reasons:

1- US military action in Somalia against Muslims
2- US tolerance of Russian atrocities against Chechnyan Muslims
3- US support of Indian oppression of Kashmiri Muslims
4- US support of Israel, particularly in conflicts against Muslims in Lebanon
5- The presence of US troops in Saudi Arabia
6- The devastating sanctions against Iraq

Bin Laden considered his attack on America to be a defensive action. In his perspective, America had declared war on Islam. He believed Muslims needed to join together to defeat America. He had a paranoid notion that the West was trying to destroy Islam since the Crusades in the Middle Ages (Figure 26). The truth is, the majority of intrusions by the West in the Middle East before 9/11 were about the Cold War conflict between Liberalism and Communism and oil. Bin Laden believed an elaborate fiction that his religion was the cause for foreign intervention, that he was a warrior in God's plan to Islamize the planet.

It is important to understand the motivation of your enemy.

You can imagine silly, untrue things about them, but in war, you have to understand the mind and purposes of your enemy. You have to understand why they make the decisions they do to predict their actions and respond accordingly. Bin Laden profoundly misunderstood America, and Americans deeply misunderstood bin Laden.

Figure 26. Crusades in the Middle Ages

Bin Laden justified the attacks against civilians because, in the grievances listed earlier, he accused America of murdering civilians. He reasoned that because America is a democracy, that all Americans are to blame for their government's actions. The truth is, most Americans are not very aware of their own government's foreign policy.

Bin Laden may have had valid criticisms of American foreign policy. He may have been right to bring these issues to the attention of Americans. However, murdering 2,977 people did not have the effect he wanted it to. Bin Laden made an error by completely misunderstanding Americans. Bin Laden expected America to cower and give him what he asked for. Instead of making Americans aware of bin Laden's grievances, Americans became aware of bin Laden. Instead of addressing bin Laden's concerns, America was ready to address bin Laden. Once he attacked innocent people, no one was interested in his motivations. He was just a psychopathic murderer who needed to be stopped at all costs. America was ready to take down bin Laden, and most of the world supported it.

Politics or Religion?

There is a debate that never seems to get resolved. The question is: Does terrorism come from politics, or does it come from religious fanaticism? That's a question that never gets answered, because it's the wrong question. For people like Osama bin Laden, there is no separation between politics and religion. The notion of separating religion and state as different things is a Western idea. To Al-Qaeda, religion and politics are inseparable. Jihad means religious war, and that is what they are waging. They believe that God is guiding them. Bin Laden listed many political grievances, but they all had a religious component. They were worldly, but he believed that these grievances were an affront to God.

During the American Civil War, there was a claim by both sides that "God is on our side." President Abraham Lincoln is alleged to have said that the statement misses the point. We don't want God to be on our side, we want to be on God's side.

The terrorists of Al-Qaeda did what they did with a clean conscience. They believed what they did was good and what God wanted them to do. That certainty is why 19 hijackers were able to kill themselves and thousands of others without any fear. A person who is absolutely certain that they are right can be very dangerous.

Movies

United 93 (2006)

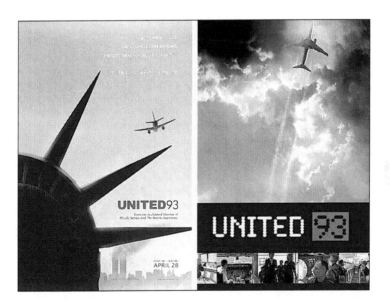

A real-time account of the events on United Flight 93, one of the planes hijacked on September 11, 2001, that crashed near Shanksville, Pennsylvania.

Directed by: Paul Greengrass

Starring: Christian Clemenson and Cheyenne Jackson

World Trade Center (2006)

On September 11, 2001, after the terrorist attack on the WTC, the building crumbled over the rescue team from the Port Authority Police Department. Will Jimeno and his sergeant John McLoughlin are found alive stuck under the wreckage while the rescue teams fight to save them.

Directed by: Oliver Stone

Starring: Nicolas Cage, Michael Peña, Maggie Gyllenhaal, Maria Bello, Stephen Dorff, Jay Hernandez, and Michael Shannon

2.3 AFTERMATH OF THE SEPTEMBER 11 ATTACKS

Figure 27. Destroyed mullions are the only thing left standing

The news played the video of the airplanes crashing into the skyscrapers over and over again. Kids at school didn't go to class. They gathered and watched the news in their classrooms live. People didn't go to work. Anyone who had a friend or family member in New York called them to make sure they were safe. The world seemed to stop briefly. In the weeks after, the only thing anyone wanted to talk about was 9/11.

Americans did not understand why it happened. They couldn't understand why somebody would do this, even though bin Laden told everyone. The reason he had attacked the US was due to American foreign policy and his own false beliefs that Islam was under attack. Even still, most people couldn't fathom why someone would do something so horrible.

Bin Laden believed that America was weak-willed and quick to give up. He believed that the dramatic experience of his attack would cause America to fold and surrender immediately. Despite his previous relationship with America, he clearly did not understand Americans.

Everywhere you went, you could see flags on cars and in front of homes. People put up American flags in front of their homes. People wore flags on their clothes. Everyone unified and sent a clear message that America wasn't going to be messed with. The Democrats and Republicans set aside their usual fights, for the time being, to focus on their common identity as Americans and to fight whoever attacked their shared country.

America did not have any interest in surrendering. Most Americans were completely uninterested in Osama bin Laden's motives at all. Young Americans signed up in tremendous numbers for military duty, eager to take the fight to Al-Qaeda.

2.3.1 INTERLUDE: WHAT'S TERRORISM?

We can't talk about a war on terror without talking about what terrorism is.

Terrorism is violence purposely targeting civilians to create fear for political ends.

A civilian is a person who isn't in the military. Civilians are not in the Army, Navy, Marines, or Air Force. Most people are civilians. Nurses, mechanics, gardeners, electricians, truck drivers, and everybody else is a civilian. Terrorists attack civilians, people who are not soldiers.

"Politics" refers to whatever the government does. The government chooses policies. Policies are the decisions about how the government wants to handle problems.

So, taking all that information and adding it up, terrorism is attacking ordinary people who aren't in the military because they want to scare the government into doing what the terrorist wants them to do.

Terrorism requires killing innocent people on purpose so that people feel terrified and do what their attackers want them to do.

Terrorism isn't new. We see it throughout history:

1913: Members of the Women's Social and Political Union (WSPU) attempted the demolition of the home of the Chancellor of the Exchequer, Lloyd George, while he was inside of it. This was part of a broader terror campaign of arson and bombings with the goal of women's suffrage in England.

1920: Forty were killed, and over 100 others were injured by a bomb delivered by a horse-drawn carriage in New York's Financial District. It is believed the attack was committed by Italian socialist anarchists.

1969: A member of the Ulster Protestant Volunteers suicide-bombed a power station in Ballyshannon, Ireland.

1963: The Ku Klux Klan planted more than a dozen sticks of dynamite with a timer beneath a black church (Figure 28). The explosion killed four young girls and wounded 22 other people. The KKK was founded as a domestic terror group after the fall of the Confederacy.

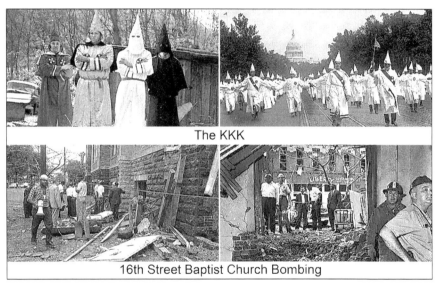
The KKK

16th Street Baptist Church Bombing

Figure 28. The KKK and the bombing of 16th Street Baptist Church

These are just a few acts of terrorism from the last century.

Terrorism is a tactic. It's a tactic that doesn't know any ideology. It has been used by anarchists, Communists, Catholics, abolitionists, nationalists, Protestants, socialists, suffragettes, and nearly any other group you can imagine.

Because terrorism is a tactic, it is a way of using violence to win a conflict. Terrorism is almost always used by people who don't have strong militaries. A country with a strong military doesn't have to attack civilians. They can take the fight to the enemy military and win in a head-on battle. Terrorists usually do not have tanks, armored personnel carriers, bombers, and interesting technologies.

Terrorists are sneaky, and they attack targets that can't fight back. If they tried to start a fight with a country like the United States, they would get crushed quickly. They understand this, and that's why they use terrorism.

It's important to understand that there is a difference between terrorism and accidental civilian casualties. War is full of tragedy, and that includes the death of civilians by accident. Stray bullets can hit an innocent person who wasn't fighting anybody. Bombs can explode and hurt innocent people. The difference is that terrorists hurt innocent people on purpose. Accidental civilian casualties are an accident but a reality of modern war.

There are painstaking efforts taken by powerful militaries to reduce civilian casualties as much as possible because we don't ever want to kill an innocent person. There's also a practical reason, which is that we don't want to turn innocent people into our enemies.

All modern militaries have something called rules of engagements, or ROE for short. These are the rules about when soldiers are allowed to start shooting or bombing. Modern soldiers are not allowed just to attack people for no reason. When they break the rules, they can find themselves inside of a military court. This is just like a civilian court, but it has different rules. If a soldier is caught breaking the rules of engagement and hurting civilians when it isn't necessary, they can find themselves in prison, just like any other criminal.

Terrorists do not share these principles. They kill innocent people deliberately. They believe that by doing so, they are doing the right thing. They don't see what they do as evil. Terrorists think that killing innocent people is the right thing to do because their cause is important.

The ways that we fight terrorism are very different from the ways that previous wars have been fought. Most wars have been fought on battlefields where the opposing forces were dressed in different uniforms and used different equipment. In most wars, it is easy for soldiers to know who their enemy is.

Soldiers wear camouflage to blend in with their environment. They use green patterns to conceal themselves in jungles, and they use tan and brown when they are covering themselves in a desert. But what if you want to conceal yourself in a city? You could use gray colors or brick colors. But what if you want to hide in plain sight? The best way to do that is to wear jeans and a t-shirt. Instead of using clothes to match nature, you use other people as the environment. You dress to match other people.

2.3.2 CHANGES IN THE HOMELAND

There were many blatant failures between Ramzi Yousef's attack in 1993 and the much more deadly re-do by 19 hijackers in 2001. There was a common saying after that day: "9/11 Changed Everything." It's not exactly true, but it did change a lot.

Homeland Security Created

Figure 29. President Bush enacts the Homeland Security Act, DHS Headquarters and seal of the DHS

You remember that before the 9/11 attacks, the CIA, FBI, and NSA all made terrible mistakes by not communicating with each other, sharing crucial information, or keeping in touch with airline security. President Bush enacted the Homeland Security Act (Figure 29), creating an organization of the same name, the Department of Homeland Security (DHS), to create a broader organization to connect 187 different federal agencies under one roof. They also created the Transportation Security Administration (TSA), a new security organization that would work inside all airports to guarantee that no one could ever slip through the border again.

The FBI and CIA were not folded into DHS, and they still maintain their independence. The White House insisted on a new policy where these agencies would be required to communicate and share information.

The security that we use now whenever we go to the airport is because of 9/11. The security is much stricter, and the line waits are much longer than they were in 2000.

The PATRIOT Act: October 26, 2001

This law gave the government new powers, some of which were controversial. For one, the law allowed for the indefinite detention of non-citizens suspected of terrorism. It gave law enforcement the power to search a home or business without telling the owner. It gave the FBI new powers to look at telephone records, emails, and financial records, without a warrant. It also gave them the right to search people's library records. Some of these powers were later struck down as unconstitutional. The law was supposed to be temporary. But the War on Terror isn't temporary. Many parts were set to expire in 2005, but Congress kept extending it. It wasn't until 2020 that the law was finally allowed to expire.

President Bush Signs **The Patriot Act** In 2001

Demonstrations Against **The Patriot Act**

Figure 30. President Bush signs the Patriot Act and demonstrations against the Patriot Act

Americans' feelings on this law were mixed. Some felt that Americans were being treated like criminals by their own government and were concerned that the government might not use the laws fairly or responsibly (Figure 30). Others felt that the law was necessary to find terrorists, and this would be a temporary provision that could be repealed once Al-Qaeda was defeated.

Domestic Surveillance: December 16, 2005

The *New York Times* reported that the NSA had been collecting data on Americans without warrants. In the US, police and federal agents are required to have a warrant signed by a judge who believes there is a reasonable suspicion of a crime before they can affect a search. Police and agents need evidence before they can search a person's home or arrest someone.

The NSA was collecting "metadata" in bulk from American phone calls. Metadata could include who called who, where they called from, how long they spoke, and when they spoke. The NSA argued that this was not a violation of the American's rights to secure their persons and property from the 4th Amendment.

This issue wouldn't be decided until the Supreme Court ruled on the case in 2015. They determined that the NSA was violating American's rights, and the NSA was ordered to cease the collection of metadata unless they could get a warrant.

Besides metadata, many other allegations were going around that the NSA monitored citizens' internet traffic, internet searches, credit-card transactions, and anything else on the internet that they could get their hands on. The NSA wanted as much information as they could get, hoping that somewhere in this immense amount of information would be clues to help them find any terrorists in the US and abroad.

3. THE WAR ON TERROR BEGINS
SEPTEMBER 14, 2001

Figure 31. US Armed Forces

Just three days after the 9/11 attacks, Congress swiftly passed The Authorization for the Use of Military Force Against Terrorists (AUMF). This was not an ordinary declaration of war. The AUMF authorized the President to use the Armed Forces against those responsible for the September 11 attacks. It also allowed the President to use all necessary and appropriate force against any nation, organization, or person that he determines planned, authorized, committed, or aided the terrorist attacks. This authorization was unprecedented. Congress gave the President the ability to attack anyone, using his best judgment.

Most of the world was on America's side. Other political issues and considerations were set aside for a moment.

3.1 CURVEBALL

Colin Powell's UN Security Council Presentation About Iraq's **WMD**

Rafid Ahmed Al-Janabi **"Curveball"**

Figure 32. Colin Powell's UN Security Council presentation about Iraq's WMD and Rafid Ahmed Al-Janabi "Curveball"

While the war in Afghanistan was already underway, the Bush administration was already building a case against the Ba'athist government of Iraq. They reached out to the UN Security Council with some chilling US intelligence. Through German sources, the CIA had made contact with an Iraqi informant, codenamed "Curveball." This anonymous man claimed that he was a chemical weapons engineer who worked for Saddam Hussein to develop mobile biological weapons labs hidden inside of vans so that they could evade UN weapons inspections.

It wasn't until much later that the world learned that Curveball was a liar. He didn't see any chemical or biological weapons being developed. He didn't work for any chemical engineering team for the government. He wasn't even a chemical engineer. He worked for a TV production company and fled Iraq because he had warrants for stealing from them. He fled to Germany and invented a story about weapons, hoping that being an informant would get him a fast track to citizenship. He finally admitted this, but not until 2011. He did not expect his lie to start a war.

As it turns out, the CIA had no assets in Iraq at the time. They had no eyes in the region. Any intelligence on the region was accepted too easily.

In addition, the White House repeatedly implied that Saddam Hussein was somehow involved with 9/11 and Al-Qaeda. An ally of the terror group that attacked America was complicit and had to be stopped.

It wasn't until many years later that a commission deeply investigated 9/11 and the Iraq War, and it came out that these ties were not real. The evidence was very thin. There's no doubt that Saddam was involved in financing terrorism. His military was developing car bombs and other weapons. However, the terrorism he financed was primarily targeting his people and Israel. There was no relationship between Saddam Hussein and Osama bin Laden.

At the same time that Curveball was lying to the government, the *New York Times* had sources within the government telling them the same information. The *New York Times* printed Curveball's lies, but the claims were given extra credibility as they came from *NYT*'s "anonymous government sources." Americans who read the news were also being lied to with information passing through leakers and the news.

3.2 MORE ATTACKS IN AMERICA

Sadly, 9/11 wasn't the last attack by Islamist terrorists. Inspired by Al-Qaeda, many more attacks followed. Many were foiled before anyone was hurt, but some did get through. Terrorists were always sure to remind the West that they weren't gone and their work wasn't finished. This isn't a complete list, but these are some of the most memorable events.

The Shoe Bomber

December 22, 2001: American Airlines Flight 63 took aboard Richard Reid, who was traveling between Paris and Miami. He had placed explosives inside of his shoes to sneak them aboard. When passengers aboard saw him trying to detonate the bomb, they attacked him and restrained him. He was arrested and given three life sentences. He was a convert to Islam who had been radicalized in Pakistan, where he was recruited by Al-Qaeda. To this day, 20 years later, people are still required to remove their shoes at airport security to put them through the x-ray machine.

Beltway Sniper Attacks

February 16–October 24, 2002: A sniper began targeting people in the Washington DC area, seemingly at random. He sent strange letters to the police claiming that he was God. It wasn't until later that the police discovered there wasn't one sniper, but two were working together: John Allen Muhammad and his 17-year-old protégé, Lee Boyd Malvo (Figure 33). They murdered 17 people before they were caught.

Figure 33. Beltway murderer John Muhammad and accomplice Lee Boyd Malvo, and the car used in the attacks

The 7/7 London Subway bombings

July 7, 2005: Three terrorists detonated bombs aboard different trains throughout London at roughly the same time in a coordinated attack. A fourth terrorist detonated a bomb on a double-decker bus (Figure 34).

Fifty-six were killed, and 784 were injured.

Two weeks later, bombers attempted a similar attack, but this time their bombs failed. Members of the terror cell were caught on camera fleeing the scene and were ultimately arrested and given life sentences. A terror cell is a small team of terrorists as a squad.

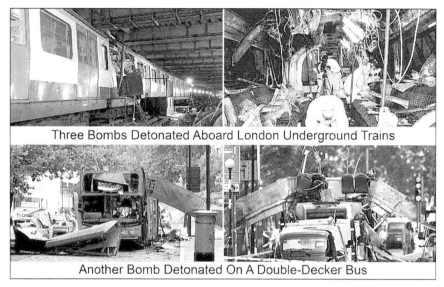

Three Bombs Detonated Aboard London Underground Trains

Another Bomb Detonated On A Double-Decker Bus

Figure 34. Three bombs detonated aboard London Underground trains and another bomb detonated on a double-decker bus

Fort Hood Mass Shooting

November 5, 2009: A US Army Major and psychiatrist named Nidal Hasan—who was stationed at Fort Hood military base near Killeen, Texas—went on a rampage (Figure 35). He killed 13 and wounded 32 fellow soldiers. Hasan was shot and, as a result, paralyzed from the waist down. It was the deadliest shooting on an American military base. Investigators later learned that he had sworn allegiance to the mujahideen and wanted to be martyred.

Hasan's comrades had been aware of his growing radicalization for several years. The disappointing failure to avoid the shootings led the Department of Defense and the FBI to authorize investigations and Congress to hold hearings.

Figure 35. US Army Major Nidal Hasan, Fort Hood Military Base, a victim being transported and Pvt. Savannah Green embraced

Underwear Bomber

December 25, 2009: On Christmas day, Umar Farouk Abdulmutallab failed to explode a Northwest Airlines plane with 289 people inside it. He had plastic explosives hidden inside his underwear. The device malfunctioned. Instead of exploding, it simply set his pants on fire. The crew rushed to put his pants out with a fire extinguisher. He didn't kill anyone, but he did give himself 2nd-degree burns on his private parts. Later investigation revealed that he was wearing a bomb that he got in Yemen. He admitted to working for Al-Qaeda. He's serving several life sentences.

Boston Marathon Bombing

April 15, 2013: During the Boston Marathon of 2013, two bombs built from pressure cookers were detonated at the finish line, where most people were gathered together (Figure 36). Three people died, and 264 people were injured. The city went on a complete lockdown. The streets were filled with police armed like they were going to war, going house to house, looking for the bombers.

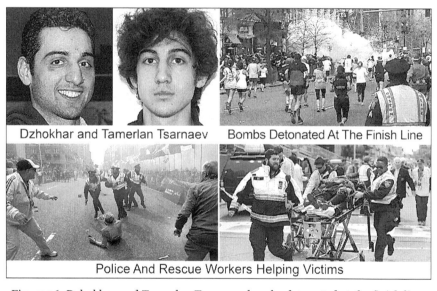

Figure 36. Dzhokhar and Tamerlan Tsarnaev, bombs detonated at the finish line, and police & rescue workers helping victims

Two days later, they were found: two brothers, Dzhokhar and Tamerlan Tsarnaev. When they were found, the brothers opened fire on the police. Tamerlan was shot several times and died soon after. Dzhokhar tried carrying his brother to an SUV to escape but was caught. Dzhokhar is on death row. They were inspired by Anwar Al-Awlaki, a well-known Al-Qaeda preacher who released content on the internet.

Movies

Patriots Day (2016)

The story of the April 15, 2013, Boston Marathon bombing, the resulting chaos, and the aftermath. Police Sgt Tommy Saunders (Mark Wahlberg) joins forces with the FBI to get to the bottom of this attack, including a city-wide search to find the terrorists responsible.

Directed by: Peter Berg

Starring: Mark Wahlberg, Kevin Bacon, John Goodman, J. K. Simmons, and Michelle Monaghan

Four Lions (2010)

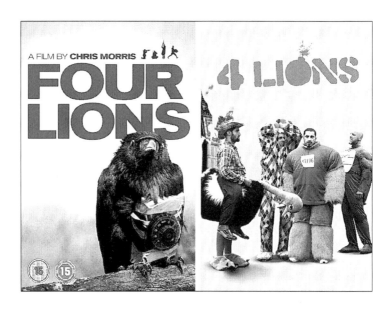

Four Lions tells the story of a group of British jihadists who push their dreams of splendor to the breaking point. As the wheels burst off and their competing ideologies collide, what arises is an emotionally appealing farce. In a storm of razor-sharp verbal banter and large-scale set pieces, Four Lions shows that while terrorism is about ideology, it can also be about idiots.

Directed by: Chris Morris

Starring: Riz Ahmed, Kayvan Novak, Nigel Lindsay, Arsher Ali, and Adeel Akhtar

4. AFGHANISTAN BEFORE OPERATION ENDURING FREEDOM

Figure 37. Map of Afghanistan

Afghanistan is a well-known difficult country to conquer and rule. Many empires have tried and failed, which is how the region earned its nickname "Graveyard of Empires."

The British Empire had a war in Afghanistan from 1839-1842. They learned that it is easier to do business with the locals, especially leaders with popular support, than fighting them. Propping up an unpopular government is a waste of money. Unpopular governments don't last long in Afghanistan. Attempts by foreign powers to rule Afghanistan in a top-down manner are always failures.

Afghanistan is situated at a crucial intersection between many regions that had vast empires: Iran and India. Afghanistan has been invaded many times by those who wanted to control the strategically valuable area. Many tribes have come into the area and made it their home, and they are not always friendly with each other. There are many old grudges in Afghanistan.

Because Afghanistan tends to have weak, dysfunctional governments, and tribalism and feuding are so common, villages and even houses are self-sufficient and are built to repel attacks. Qalats, which means "fortifications," are everywhere.

Figure 38. Afghanistan's mountainous and jagged terrain

Afghanistan is geologically very challenging. The terrain is mountainous and jagged (Figure 38). Traveling by ground is very difficult. There are also countless cave networks, unmapped and unknown to people who don't live in the region.

Caves can be used as places to hide, places to stage ambushes, and a way to move stealthily without being detected by satellites or drones.

Afghanistan has seen many, many empires: the Indian Kingdom of Gandhara, the Achaemenid Persian Empire, the Maurya Empire, the Greeks, the Mongols, the Mughals (Figure 39). It has been divided into feuding smaller nations and empires, usually forged from the remnants of an empire that retreated or collapsed: Scythians, Greco-Bactrians, Hephthalites, Indo-Parthians, the Kushans, and Kidarites.

Arabs first inhabited the region at the start of the 8th century. Even back then, Afghanistan was well-known as a tough place, full of small tribes who weren't afraid of a fight. Early attempts at conquest failed miserably. It took nearly 200 years for Islam to be fully adopted in Afghanistan, culminating after Iran conquered Kabul. However, the Hindu dynasty, the Shahi, resisted conquest and conversion for another 100 years after that.

The Mongol Empire, which swept through the world, quickly overrunning their adversaries wherever they went, was hindered by the people in Afghanistan. Mongols attempted intimidation and butchery, but the Afghan people weren't impressed. As they always did, they held out long enough to watch the empire crumble and recede.

The Mughals managed to take and hold Kabul for twenty years before conquering India; the Mughal held onto the Hindu Kush region until 1738. They kept control of a few urban areas, and they basically ignored the rest of the region or simply paid them off to make them happy. Despite that, they were constantly dealing with tribal revolts.

The Mughal Empire lost its territory in Afghanistan to the Persian Safavids. The new rulers had to deal with the same problems that every other would-be conqueror had. The tribal revolts brought down the Safavids, same as every other empire that thought it was better than the previous tenant. The modern nation of Afghanistan was founded in 1747, but this rulership mainly existed on paper. Many tribes are ethnically distinct and unfriendly to one another. Calling the region a country is fiction.

Figure 39. Afghanistan's ancient rulers: Arabs, Mongols, Mughals and Persian Safavids

The Afghanistan region has an ancient tradition of being invaded by large, powerful, foreign countries. Every single time, the Afghans make their lives as difficult as possible and simply wait it out. The people of Afghanistan have been doing this for 2,500 years. In the 1980s, the Soviet Union (USSR) had to relearn the same lesson.

Proxy War

After WWII, the United States had the most potent, terrifying weapon ever created in its arsenal: the atomic bomb. Immediately after WWII, former allies, the US and the Soviet Union, quickly became enemies. Their alliance was to defeat Nazi Germany. With Germany defeated, they had no reason to be friends. The two countries had very different philosophies. The Soviet Union's ideology required a global worker's revolution. It wasn't enough that they were Communists. They had to spread Communism across the world, whether others wanted it or not.

When the Soviet Union developed its own atomic bomb, the war changed forever. No two nuclear-armed countries have ever gone to war with one another. Between the end of WWII and the fall of the Soviet Union (1945-1989), the US and the Soviet Union engaged in what was named the "Cold War." Any conflict between the United States and the USSR was waged by proxy.

The Cold War was, in large part, a series of proxy wars. A proxy is a person who is acting on behalf of another person. A proxy war is when a country finances, supplies, and supports one side of a conflict between two other countries. They pick sides in the war and try to help the country they support without getting directly involved by sending in troops or firing weapons. The US and the Soviet Union never fought each other directly. They supplied and aided other countries that went to war with each other.

The worry since the 1950s has been that if two countries with nuclear weapons ever go to war, one or both might use those nuclear weapons. No one wants to risk nuclear war. In a proxy war, the countries could help in a conflict without directly participating. It's a buffer against the conflict escalating into a hot war. A hot war between two nations with nuclear weapons could mean the extinction of the human species.

The second reason is that people don't like war. During wars, people have friends, relatives, and coworkers who leave to go to battle. Some of them come back wounded or maimed. Some come back psychologically hurt. Many come back in caskets draped in the flag of their country. In a proxy war, you can still conduct a war, but the country's citizens don't pay as close attention as they would if their own family and friends were involved.

During the Cold War, a war could hardly happen on earth without the US choosing one side and the Soviet Union choosing the other side, both of them giving aid, money, training, and supplies, and hoping that their side would win.

The United States was on the receiving end of a proxy war in Vietnam from 1963 to 1973. Vietnam was entangled in a civil war, and the conflict split the country into two, with the northern half adopting Communism and the southern half remaining friendly to the West (Figure 40). America participated directly in this war to assist the South in stopping Communism from taking over the entire country.

The Soviet Union and China also participated in the war, but not directly. They used North Vietnam as their proxy to fight the US. The Soviet Union assisted the Communists of

Figure 40. Map of North and South Vietnam

North Vietnam by giving them weapons, intelligence, and training. This strategy worked. America ultimately gave up on the war, and the Communists were able to take control of all of Vietnam.

About a decade later, the Soviet Union had its own Vietnam War, so to speak. The Soviet Union attempted to invade Afghanistan, a country that is famously difficult to wage an offensive war in. The country is large, the terrain is very mountainous, and there are countless tunnel networks to hide in. The situation was very similar to Vietnam but in reverse. The Soviets were attempting to aid the Communist government in a fight against anti-Communist Muslim mujahideen, who were supported by the US.

The United States assisted the anti-Communist Afghan militia who fought back against the Soviet invasion. These fighters were called freedom fighters by the West. The US gave them training in guerrilla warfare and gave them weapons. And just as the United States failed to secure Vietnam, the USSR failed to secure Afghanistan. The government that was backed by the USSR had no more support, and they were overthrown by the rebels. These rebels created a new regime they called The Islamic State of Afghanistan, which was overthrown by The Islamic Emirate of Afghanistan, also known as The Taliban.

Some of the mujahideen that the CIA trained and supplied would come back to haunt their former American allies. Among these mujahideen were three people who will become very important when we get to 2001:

1- Osama bin Laden: financier and leader of the terror group Al-Qaeda
2- Abu Musab Al-Zarqawi: leader of the Al-Qaeda insurgency in Iraq
3- Mullah Mohammed Omar: leader of the Taliban

Afghanistan Under the Taliban

The Taliban was a religiously fanatical government that ruled by extremely traditional interpretations of Islamic law. The Taliban was immensely brutal and cruel, using ancient punishments such as cutting off hands for petty theft and executing people for blaspheming.

They destroyed ancient artifacts if they weren't Muslim, which included dynamiting 1400-year-old statues of Buddha (Figure 41). They ransacked the National Museum of Afghanistan and destroyed thousands of ancient artifacts and sculptures. They destroyed libraries with any books they disapproved of. The Taliban effectively outlawed any form of education that wasn't religious.

Figure 41. Taliban fighters, destruction of Buddha statue, and repression of women

They abused Sikhs and Hindus and murdered Christians. Women were repressed in the extreme. These actions were condemned by governments and non-profit groups all over the world.

For a while, The Taliban permitted drug trafficking, and Afghanistan was one of the largest producers of heroin in the world. By 1999, they moved 4,000 tons of opium, which is used to make heroin. The Taliban also had legal slavery, frequently kidnapping children and forcing them to become soldiers or kidnapping girls and forcing them to marry men.

The Taliban was tolerant of terrorists. They let them come and go as they pleased and use the country as a training ground and a place to hide out. Al-Qaeda made its home in Afghanistan.

Movie

Rambo III (1988)

John Rambo joins forces with the mujahideen to fight against the Soviet Union during the Soviet-Afghan War. Near the end, Rambo gives a rousing speech where he describes the Afghan insurgents as heroic freedom fighters. This is a silly action movie that shows the positive attitude that Americans had towards Afghanistan before 9/11.

Of course, in 1988, no one had any idea what would happen in 2001.

Directed by: Peter MacDonald

Starring: Sylvester Stallone and Richard Crenna

Book

The Kite Runner by Khaled Hosseini

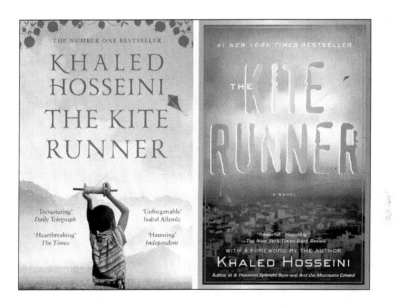

The story takes place during a lot of the history covered in this chapter, including the fall of Afghanistan's monarchy, the war with the Soviet Union, and the rise of the Taliban.

5. OPERATION ENDURING FREEDOM

Enduring Freedom is the operational name for the War on Terror. It mainly refers to actions taken in Afghanistan but also included operations in Asia and Africa.

The War on Terror was not a war on a country. The enemy was international. The war wasn't against a government. The enemy was sometimes working with governments but wasn't in control of any government.

The War on Terror was and continues to be a hunt against all terrorists of any stripe, wherever they hide, and against anyone who would give them shelter, aid, or money.

The United States organized a coalition of 60 countries that would all work together. Every member of the Coalition signed on to defeat Al-Qaeda. Not all of them had militaries strong enough to participate directly but showed their support in other ways such as intelligence sharing. The biggest members included France, the UK, Germany, and Poland.

Invasion

Coalition forces had the advantage of advanced technology and vastly greater resources. The Taliban had the advantage of knowing the land, blending in with the populace, and being a force that had a lifetime of experience with fending off foreign invaders.

The Coalition's strategy was to cut off any foreign support to the Taliban. That meant Pakistan in particular. Pakistan and India have had a turbulent relationship since it was founded. Pakistan shares a border with India and felt that they needed to remain friendly with Afghanistan to have a path westward if they had to go to war with India. Pakistan wasn't pro-Taliban; they were pro-access through Afghanistan.

Knowing this, the Coalition gave an ultimatum to Pakistan: "You're either with us, or you are with the terrorists." Pakistan formally renounced support for the Taliban four days after 9/11.

Codename Jawbreaker

The next part of the strategy was to make contact with the Northern Alliance (NA), the Taliban's only real rival in the region. Before the Taliban, the country was divided up by feuding warlords. The Taliban was the most successful, taking the majority of the country. The remaining warlords and their tribes banded together into the Northern Alliance. These were all people who had just recently been at war with one another, but they managed to set aside their differences for the time being and work together to defeat their common enemy, the Taliban.

CIA operatives reached out to the NA. If the Coalition was going to be successful, they'd need as much local support as they could get. The Coalition bought the support of the NA with $3 million.

Figure 42. Northern Alliance troops

A combined joint special operations group, Task Force Dagger, met with the NA. They gave training, weapons, and equipment to the Northern Alliance militia (Figure 42). The Coalition needed them to be ready and capable of fighting alongside Coalition forces.

October 7, 2001: Americans and Brits used superior air power to hit key Taliban and Al-Qaeda targets, at the same time as cruise missiles were fired from ships on the coast. The Coalition's bombing campaign wiped out a lot of the Taliban's military infrastructure. Very quickly, all Taliban airpower was destroyed. The Coalition won uncontested control of the skies above Afghanistan.

October 30: Special forces snuck into the Panjshir Valley to meet with the commander of the Northern Alliance. They linked up and moved through the mountains to their first target, Mazar-i-Sharif, the fourth largest city in Afghanistan.

Meanwhile, NA forces attacked Taliban forces in a feint. The point wasn't to win the engagement but to lure the Taliban forces away from the airstrip in Mazar-i-Sharif. Once the Taliban were far away chasing after NA forces, the 75th US Army Rangers airdropped in. Only one Taliban soldier was left to guard the location. The airstrip was quickly taken, and Coalition forces turned it into their forward operating base.

November 9: The attack on Mazar-i-Sharif began. Special forces used lasers to designate targets and sent coordinates to bombers and missile systems. After a day of softening the city up with long-range explosives, the NA militia invaded to handle any remaining resistance. The following battle lasted only 90 minutes. Seven hundred Taliban were killed, while the NA suffered less than 50 losses. The Taliban were on the run.

The road to Kabul, the capital, was wide open. NA militia moved in, and the Taliban couldn't offer much resistance. The Taliban held out for only three days before they were overrun. Conventional warfare was a guaranteed loss for the Taliban. They simply could not go toe-to-toe with Coalition forces.

Meanwhile, Rangers battled with Taliban camps in Kandahar.

Coalition forces owned the skies. With their new forward operating base, they could deploy anywhere they wanted, anytime they wanted, moving troops across the large country in helicopters.

November 25: The Battle of Qala-i-Jangi (close to Mazar-i-Sharif) was an unexpected fight. It started when 600 Taliban and Al-Qaeda prisoners revolted against their captors. They seized the fortress and weapons there. The revolt was quickly defeated. During the revolt, one CIA officer died, Johnny Michael Span. He was the very first American to die in the war.

November 26: Kunduz was the last city to hold out. Five thousand Taliban occupied the city. It was besieged for 12 days before they folded, and the NA and Coalition took it. Taliban forces surrendered as a whole, but there was no leadership present. The prevailing theory remains that they had been secretly airlifted out by ISI, the Pakistani intelligence organization. Pakistan had renounced the Taliban publicly, but were they still supporting them secretly? This event has been named the "Airlift of Evil."

Figure 43. Kandahar

December 6: Kandahar (Figure 43), the Taliban's last major stronghold, was battered with a campaign of ordinance and was surrounded. These defenders were the first to try negotiating with the NA and Coalition. Taliban forces in Kandahar finally surrendered on the 7th.

The Taliban regime was officially defeated. A new government was formed under the supervision of the Coalition. Hamid Karzai became the President of the transitional government

The Coalition had succeeded in deposing the Taliban, but the most important targets were nowhere to be found. Osama bin Laden, KSM, and other Al-Qaeda leadership were still at large. They may have fled during the invasion to Jalalabad. Intelligence could track bin Laden at points until he slipped away into an underground cave network in the White Mountains called Tora Bora. If bin Laden was in there, it would be extremely difficult to fish him out. Mujahideen had used those caves to significant effect against the Soviets just over ten years earlier.

The Coalition decided to rely on local Afghan troops who knew the region well. They recruited 3,000 militia and linked them with special forces to help organize them. The force entered the maze of underground tunnels. The militia was not as effective as the CIA believed it would be. They made contact with enemy forces, but it wasn't going to be a breeze. Enemy forces could appear from nowhere, attack with rifles and bombs, and slip away and vanish. After some serious fighting, the Taliban and Al-Qaeda offered a cease-fire to negotiate. This was a trick. During the negotiations, bin Laden and his crew snuck away through the tunnels, possibly to Pakistan.

The Taliban had been routed. Al-Qaeda was on the run. Afghanistan was free.

But the invasion was the easy part. As empires have learned repeatedly, for over 2,000 years, taking Afghanistan is easy—holding Afghanistan is impossible.

The Mission Changes

Taliban and Al-Qaeda knew Afghanistan's history very well. They decided to use it to their advantage.

Figure 44. George Washington and the Continental Army

Al-Qaeda's strategy was not to win. Their strategy was not to lose. That concept should be familiar to Americans because it is the same strategy we often employ, and it was used by George Washington. A small but dedicated force can make things very difficult for a much larger force using guerrilla tactics. The mighty nation can spend an outrageous amount of wealth and energy trying to defeat them. In the case of the American Revolution, George Washington never had ambitions to conquer England. He did not need to create a navy to cross the Atlantic Ocean and invade. He didn't need a force of Marines to overthrow the monarchy. He didn't need soldiers to occupy London and police the country while installing a new American government. All the Americans had to do was make the war so difficult for the English that they would decide it wasn't worth it anymore. That's exactly what George Washington and the Continental Army (Figure 44) accomplished and why America exists today.

That's the same strategy that the mujahideen used against the USSR in the 1980s. It was the same strategy that they would use against the US. The Afghan insurgents simply had to make it so difficult for the invader that the invader would give up, decide it wasn't worth all the death and money, and just go home. Insurgents in Iraq also had this strategy. If you can drag out the war for as long as possible, America will eventually tire of seeing Americans come home in wheelchairs or body bags. The insurgents need to hold out long enough and drain the occupying force of money and morale. Make no mistake. The mujahideen could be very, very patient.

Operation Anaconda

February 2002: US intelligence identifies a force of 600 Taliban and Al-Qaeda moving back into Afghanistan. Special forces are deployed to intercept them swiftly by chopper under cover of night. The Taliban had learned their lesson from the fighting that came before. This was a trap. Special forces flew right into a disaster. Their choppers touched down and realized too late that they had landed directly into a Taliban kill-zone. Special forces were attacked. Taliban hammered their Apache air support with rockets and anti-material rifles. They took down two Chinook helicopters (Figure 45). US positions were pinned down from several directions and bombarded with mortar fire. They called for backup.

Figure 45. AH-64 Apache Helicopter and CH-47 Chinook Helicopter

Local Afghan militia answered the call. They loaded up into their civilian vehicles and drove to the fight. However, this militia had decorated their trucks with brightly colored flower patterns and kept their truck's headlights on, making them easy targets to spot. The militia was decimated by Taliban fire. Although the US ultimately won the engagement, this battle revealed some weaknesses in the Coalition forces, including their poor coordination with local militias.

Only 23 Taliban bodies were found, despite believing there were as many as 600 at the start. The remaining forces likely snuck back across the border. Eight Americans were killed, and dozens were wounded.

Insurgency

From the day Coalition forces announced victory to the present day, it has been a war against insurgents, not armies. Coalition forces were now experiencing what a dozen empires before have experienced.

January 1, 2015

Operation Enduring Freedom ended. Operation Freedom's Sentinel began. The mission changed from direct action against the Taliban. The mission was now to support locals so that they could withstand the Taliban themselves.

War in Afghanistan could be described as long periods of boredom, punctuated by absolute terror. Most of the work to do was to make friends with the locals and try to get support and intelligence to help fight against the Taliban. Coalition soldiers were not diplomats. They didn't have any understanding of Afghan culture, let alone the specific practices and ways of thinking of the countless tribes in the country. The Afghan people, likewise, didn't understand foreigners.

The country is very rural. Most people live in extreme poverty. If a farmer's goat was accidentally killed by a stray bullet, it was a devastating loss to their family. Conflicts between villages and soldiers often erupted over things like dead goats or accidentally offending them. They had little information about the outside world, living very isolated lives. In some places, child abuse was considered an ordinary practice by Afghans, which made it very difficult for soldiers to set that abuse aside to cooperate with them.

Figure 46. Poppy farms

The Taliban was primarily financed by poppy farms (Figure 46), which are flowers used to make heroin. Coalition forces destroyed these crops to cut off money to the Taliban and to stop the export of drugs to other countries. The farmers who ran those farms were not necessarily Taliban themselves. Their entire farms, their livelihoods, and the ways they pay to feed their family were wiped out. These farmers often joined the Taliban just because they were angry with the Coalition for destroying their farms.

Getting any widespread cooperation among Afghan people was also seemingly impossible. Many of these tribes and villages had old grudges against each other and were not interested in cooperating. Many had hatred for the Northern Alliance, the group of warlords who oppressed them before the Taliban did.

Meanwhile, the Taliban and Al-Qaeda were waging a war that they knew very well. They hid in the craggy, cavernous, rugged terrain and made sneak attacks. When there was return fire, they dissolved back into the landscape, disappearing again.

Any error by Coalition forces was seized upon immediately. A bomb that dropped and accidentally killed civilians was used as propaganda by insurgents. They would find the relatives of the dead and promise them revenge and give them a suicide vest to seek payback against the Coalition. They waged the same kind of war against the Coalition that they waged against the Soviet Union.

The Taliban was happy to drag this fight out as long as necessary. Over the next 20 years, Taliban forces grew in strength, year after year, like the tide coming in and out. They could be stopped, but they always came back. There are soldiers stationed in Afghanistan right now, fighting a war that started before they were born.

Technology

The Coalition was decades more technologically advanced than the Taliban. The Coalition had access to cutting-edge weapons, drones, communications, airpower, body armor, and night vision goggles (NVG). The Taliban mostly worked with relics from the Cold War—weapons like AK-47s (Figure 47) that were often older than the soldiers who carried them.

Figure 47. Night vision goggles and AK-47s

Somehow, the Taliban was able to resist, despite them being so technologically behind. How is that possible?

Whenever a new technology is developed, enemies quickly figure it out and create an identical technology or develop countermeasures for it. Any military technology developed will be obsolete within a couple of years. New weapon systems and technologies have to be continuously created to be one step ahead. The idea isn't to get lightyears ahead in technology. That's impossible. The military just wants to be one year more technologically developed than their enemies.

In the early days of the war, insurgents were fond of using cell phone bombs, an improvised explosive device (IED) to attack Coalition forces from a distance. They would attach any cell phone to a bomb and hide it somewhere. A scout would watch the bomb and wait for an enemy force to move past it. When the enemy was close enough, the insurgent would simply call the phone attached to the bomb, which detonated the bomb remotely. The United States developed a way to stop these by cranking out a high-powered radio signal from trucks. It created a zone where the radio waves were so strong that any radio waves from cell phones couldn't get through. The bombers figured this out and moved on to different ways to attack. IEDs became less usable, but Coalition forces had to spend a ton of money to develop and outfit vehicles with them. Insurgents moved on to other ways to blow people up.

The night vision systems have improved a lot during the War on Terror. Over and over again, insurgents found ways to beat night vision systems in very clever ways, requiring updates to Coalition NVG systems. In 20 years, the NVGs used by the military were extremely powerful and very expensive.

6. THE 10-YEAR HUNT FOR BIN LADEN

On March 1, 2003, KSM, the mastermind of the 9/11 attack, was found and arrested. He was housed inside a military prison, where he became a valuable source of information for the Coalition. Much of what we now know about the lead-up to the 9/11 attacks came from KSM himself. He also took credit for several other acts of terrorism. He is still in prison to this day, awaiting an execution trial. However, there has been some argument in his case that he may have been forced to confess under force. The CIA was notoriously known to have used some controversial methods to find bin Laden and other Al-Qaeda leadership.

The CIA used techniques they described as "extraordinary rendition" or "enhanced interrogation" on prisoners of war. The world learned about a practice called "waterboarding." A prisoner is laid on their back on a plank of wood and tied to it. A towel is put over their face, and water is poured over them. The effect is that the victim experiences the sensation of drowning. This is a terrifying thing to endure. Prisoners were also forced to take "stress positions," extremely uncomfortable postures. When Americans learned about these practices, there was a worldwide debate on whether these count as torture or if they were justified.

The CIA also set up fake vaccination drives. This was a hoax. The true goal was to collect genetic samples from people who came to use their services. They then ran these samples of DNA against databases of terrorists.

Bin Laden was not found using these methods. The CIA found him using good old-fashioned wiretaps, human intelligence (HUMINT), and computer hacking.

It took ten years to finally find bin Laden. He was discovered in Pakistan, not Afghanistan. By then, Bush was no longer the President. The job of fighting the War on Terror was now the job of President Barack Obama (Figure 48).

Figure 48. US President Barack Obama

The US lost track of bin Laden at Tora Bora. He'd escaped through an old smuggler's route that had been used since ancient times.

Bin Laden was living in luxury in an enormous compound built for him in 2003-2005 in Abbottabad (Figure 49). It stuck out like a sore thumb and was by far the largest and most luxurious building in the area, located less than a mile from the Pakistan Military Academy. Allegedly, the compound was used as a safe house by ISI. We don't know for sure, but it is suspected by many that bin Laden was kept under house arrest by Pakistani Inter-Services Intelligence (ISI).

Despite never leaving the house and never using phones, bin Laden still maintained communication to his terror network using couriers—very simple intermediaries between him and his lieutenants, like his own private mail carrier. Using several couriers helped to keep his location secret.

Al-Qaeda was savvy enough not to show themselves over the phone or the internet. They relied on couriers to deliver messages. CIA hackers secretly attacked Al-Qaeda computers and installed surveillance software onto the phones of those couriers. After that, they could easily track courier movements and communications and map the courier network.

In 2010, US intelligence caught a suspect using the fake name Abu Ahmed Al-Kuwaiti on a wiretap. That wiretap traced him to that compound in Abbottabad. Once they had a lead on him and focused intelligence gathering there, they learned about the compound. After watching it, they noticed that only two people ever visited it: Al-Kuwaiti and his brother. They had access to the compound and easily came and went. They were the key members of the courier network, the only two people from outside the compound that ever made contact with whoever was inside.

The CIA watched the building like a hawk. Using aerial drones, intelligence saw someone on the roof that would go for walks on the rooftop alone. They called him "Pacer." They suspected that this man was Osama bin Laden, but they didn't know for sure.

Figure 49. Bin Laden's compound in Abbottabad

Neptune Spear

Because they thought ISI might have been involved with the man in the compound, there was no way to ask for Pakistan's help in capturing Pacer. Any bombing was off the table too, since it would risk civilian casualties and make it impossible to identify who Pacer is. Instead, they opted for a commando raid without any contact with the government of Pakistan.

Twenty-three operators were selected from Seal Team 6. These are elite soldiers of the highest level of skill and competence. The military built perfect replicas of the compound in Virginia and Nevada. The team trained for months there, practicing maneuvers over and over until they knew it by heart. They were hoping that Pacer was bin Laden and they were not going to leave anything to chance.

April 28: The team was ready. They arrived in Jalalabad.

This operation was extremely risky. If the US raided a building in Pakistan and Pacer was not bin Laden, it could be an international incident. The White House was willing to take that chance.

May 2: 11 pm, Seals boarded a pair of custom-modified stealth Black Hawks (Figure 50). They departed 50 miles from Tora Bora, where bin Laden had escaped Coalition forces almost ten years earlier. Onboard these Black Hawks were 23 Seals, one Pakistani-American translator, and one Belgian military dog.

Two more choppers containing 25 more Seals were held in reserve nearby, just in case something went wrong. The mission might have gone bad, or worse; the Pakistani military could interfere in the operation and attack the first Seal group.

1:30 am, the Seal team made a final approach to the compound. Suddenly, sirens and alarms went off in Helicopter One. There was a technical malfunction. It had to make an emergency landing. The chopper went over the wall and crashed right onto the lawn inside the compound. Helicopter Two touched down across the street. Seals from Helicopter One reported that no one had been injured. Despite this, they continued the mission as planned.

Wearing night-vision goggles, a 12-man team from Helicopter One breached the gate to the compound. Helicopter Two's team secured the perimeter and entered from the north of the compound. A small team from Helicopter One moved towards the guest house, while the main group split up into smaller teams to clear the main compound.

Figure 50. Black Hawk helicopter and custom-modified stealth Black Hawk helicopter

The guest house was occupied by the courier Al-Kuwaiti and his family. When he went for a gun, the Seals shot and killed him.

At the same time, Seals entered the 1st floor of the main building, where they encountered Al-Kuwaiti's brother and fellow courier, Abrar, and his wife and kids. After a short gunfight, both Abrar and his wife were killed.

On every floor, the stairs were blocked with iron gates. They all had to be destroyed with explosive C4 charges.

On their way up to the 2nd floor, seals made contact with Khalid, bin Laden's 23-year-old son, who was armed. Seals got him immediately, and he was shot dead.

On the 3rd floor, they found a tall thin man peeking through a door.

Three Seals burst in. Inside the room were three women. Two of them put themselves between the Seals and the tall man, making a human shield. They were two of his wives. One of the wives was shot in the leg. The other two were tackled by Seals, who were worried they might have been wearing suicide vests.

At the same time, a Seal fired at the man. Over the radio, he called it in, "For God and country. Geronimo. Geronimo. Geronimo." Geronimo was the code word used to communicate that an enemy was killed.

Four men and one woman were killed in the raid, none of them American.

For 20 minutes, the Seals searched the compound for anything that could be used for intelligence, such as computers, flash drives, and phones. Meanwhile, a demolition charge was attached to the chopper to destroy it so that it couldn't fall into enemy hands.

One of the Chinooks in reserve was deployed to pick up the Seals who had lost their ride home. They brought along the body of the tall man they'd killed. Intelligence confirmed that this was bin Laden.

May 1, 2011, at 11:30 pm: Obama announced Osama bin Laden, the leader of Al-Qaeda, was dead. His body was buried at sea at a never disclosed location.

Movie

Zero Dark Thirty (2012)

An action thriller about the hunt for bin Laden and the raid on his compound.

For several years, CIA operative Maya is single-minded in her hunt for leads to discover the whereabouts of Al-Qaeda's leader, Osama Bin Laden. Lastly, in 2011, it seems that her work will pay off, and a US Navy SEAL team is sent to kill or arrest Bin Laden. But only Maya is sure Bin Laden is where she says he is.

Directed by: Kathryn Bigelow

Starring: Jessica Chastain, Jason Clarke, Joel Edgerton, Reda Kateb, Kyle Chandler, and Jennifer Ehle

7. IRAQ BEFORE THE WAR ON TERROR

Figure 51. Map of Iraq

Iraq is a country with a history of instability, internal conflict, and war. For 24 years, the only thing holding it together was the iron fist of the dictator Saddam Hussein. Virtually no one regards Saddam with fondness. He made enemies with all of his neighbors, his people, and the international community. But without his presence, Iraq would have lost the one person holding everything together. If Iraq was a Jenga tower, Saddam was the pulled piece that made it collapse.

In 1918, the Ottoman Empire was on the losing side of World War I. The winners of that war divided up the Ottoman territory into new territories. Those new borders account for what is most of the Middle East today. Britain and France simply drew new borders and allocated responsibility between one another for the new countries they had just created from thin air.

This is how the nation of Iraq came to be, with Britain taking responsibility for it. The British chose Sunni Arabs to run the country, despite the majority of the country being Shiite. This was a classic trick that the British Empire used in many of their colonies. When Britain invaded a foreign country, they would find a minority group within the nation and hand them power. As a disempowered minority group, they were often grateful. In addition, the new minority group in power would want to keep Britain in charge, fearful that if the British left, the majority of the country would come for them and seek revenge.

Britain decided that the new nation of Iraq would be a monarchy, and they chose a man named Faisal I (Figure 52) to be the king. He was a member of a powerful dynasty, a royal family from Jordan. He had briefly declared himself the king of Syria the year before, but the French removed him almost immediately. He lived in Britain for a year until they offered to let him be the king of Iraq. Despite already failing to be king of Syria, Faisal gave it another shot.

Faisal I ruled as the king of Iraq for fourteen years. In 1932, he requested independence from Britain, and Britain accepted. The plan was to allow the countries to grow into their own so that they would eventually not need foreign support. Iraq became its own independent nation.

Figure 52. Faisal I bin Al-Hussein bin Ali Al-Hashemi

Many Iraqis were not pleased with the king because he was a member of a foreign family, the Hashemites. In 1941, as WWII was in full swing, a group of his advisors calling themselves The Golden Square organized a coup. They failed to overthrow King Faisal II, the grandson of the previous king, but it became clear that Iraq was not yet a stable nation.

The period between 1952-1970 was called the Arab Cold War. There was a conflict in the Arab world between the new, secular nationalist governments and the traditionalist monarchies. In 1958, during the July Revolution, King Faisal II was overthrown by the new leader of Iraq, Prime Minister (PM) Abd Al-Karim Qasim. The new PM was a military man and a nationalist.

Saddam Hussein Abd Al-Majid Al-Tikriti (Figure 53) was born in 1937. He was anti-British and resented the colonial influence over his country and continued foreign intervention.

Figure 53. Saddam Hussein Abd Al-Majid Al-Tikriti

He was one of many in the growing movement of Arab nationalism. He dropped out of school to join the Ba'ath party. The Ba'athists shared Saddam Hussein's nationalist attitudes. They preached Arab unity and the removal of all foreign empires from the region. The Ba'athists tried to overthrow Qasim but failed. Saddam Hussein fled to Egypt by riding a donkey through the desert.

Ba'athism was an international movement trying to organize the region into an alliance against foreigners and monarchies. This movement was strong enough that there was serious talk between the Ba'athists of Syria and Egypt into unifying their countries.

Hussein didn't return to his home until 1963, when Qasim was successfully overthrown by Abdul Salam Arif and members of the Ba'ath party. The leader of the Ba'athists, Ahmed Hassan Al-Bakr, and Arif did not get along. Al-Bakr got rid of all non-Ba'athists and secured a total Ba'athist government without any challenges from other ideologies.

Saddam began working his way up the ladder. When the negotiations between Syria and Iraq's Ba'athists were split, it sent the message that the pan-Arab unity movement was weak. Arif thought the Ba'athists saw an opportunity and took it. He organized a counter-coup and once again placed himself in charge of Iraq. Ba'athists were thrown in prison, including Saddam Hussein.

Arif didn't rule for long. He died in a plane crash and was succeeded by his brother. This brother, like his brother before him, was also removed in a coup by the same man, Al-Bakr, in 1968. Many could put themselves in control of Iraq, but no one could hold onto it very long.

With Ba'athists back in power, Saddam was released from prison. Being distantly related to Al-Bakr, he was offered the job as Vice President. He took the job. This regime was not going to let another coup happen ever again. All rebels were imprisoned, tortured, executed, or all three.

7.1 IRAQ UNDER SADDAM

In 1979, the President of Iraq was getting old. Saddam took control of the military and became the de facto leader. A de facto leader is a person who isn't the official leader by law but acts as the leader anyway. President Al-Bakr slowly became little more than the public face. Eventually, Saddam persuaded Al-Bakr to retire. With the military under his control and the President's health waning, he gave Saddam the presidency. Just to make sure that no one had a problem with that, Saddam ordered the execution of many top officers and officials. He had seen a lot of coups in his lifetime and wasn't about to let any come for him.

Saddam developed a reputation for being brutal and possibly crazy. He was notoriously paranoid. Dictators tend to be paranoid. Saddam was paranoid even by those standards.

Saddam poured tons of resources into domestic spying and security, locking down the people. He used his spying agencies to spy on each other. Since failure could be punished, they often had to make things up and accuse others without proof. Those accused would be tortured until they confessed and forced to tell about accomplices. If there weren't any accomplices, the tortured person might just give them names of innocent people, who would also be arrested and tortured and forced to give names. An accusation was always a death sentence.

Meanwhile, Saddam's son Uday (Figure 54) behaved like a real-life monster. He and his private gang of Fedayeen committed unbelievably terrible crimes against people. In one case, he fed a military leader to a tiger because Uday didn't believe his salute was sincere enough. He would pick women off the streets, and his goons would kidnap them. Often, the woman was never seen again.

Figure 54. Uday Saddam Hussein

His behavior was so vile that even his father, Saddam Hussein, arrested him and seriously considered executing him. But Saddam kept giving him one more chance, again and again.

Speaking ill of the regime was also a death sentence. People never said anything against the government over the phone. People just assumed the phones were tapped. When people spoke ill of the Husseins, they did it only at home, speaking quietly to their family, just in case someone was nearby listening.

7.1.1 IRAN–IRAQ WAR

Shah Mohammad Reza Pahlavi

Ayatollah Khomeini

Figure 55. Shah Mohammad Reza Pahlavi and Ayatollah Khomeini

In 1980, Iran had just gone through a revolution. The Shah Mohammad Reza Pahlavi was removed and replaced with a religious government led by Ayatollah Khomeini. The new government was still recovering from the revolution from the year before and was unproven as a workable government. Khomeini and Hussein did not like each other at all. Khomeini was a Shiite religious fundamentalist. Saddam was a relatively secular Sunni nationalist who ruled an 80% Shiite country. He was worried that the Iranian revolution could come to Iraq and that the Shiite majority would overthrow him.

Saddam picked a piece of Iranian land in the oil-rich Khuzestan Province. The region was primarily Arab, though Iran is a predominantly Persian country. Taking this province would give Iraq access to the Shatt Al-Arab waterway, which connects the vital Tigris and Euphrates rivers and provides access to many gulf shorelines and the oil fields there.

September 22, 1980: Iraq declares a surprise attack on Iran. Saddam had no military training or experience, or even a high school diploma, yet decided to declare himself supreme commander of the military. Likely he did this because of his lifetime of experience watching military leaders overthrow the government, time and time again. Understandably, he didn't trust anyone else to run his military without using the military against him.

Saddam's strategy was to essentially line his military along the border and march them forward. It bears repeating that he had no military experience whatsoever and had no idea about how to wage war or develop a strategy. Saddam expected the new government of Iran to crumble. His invasion had the opposite effect. The people of Iran solidified against their new common enemy, Iraq.

The initial invasion was a disaster. The Iraqi military was completely disorganized, spread thin. Saddam gave them too many missions that often had conflicting objectives. Sensing that the military didn't have their heart in it, Saddam ordered the execution of any general who called a retreat. He killed three of his generals this way. Shortly after, he realized his generals were right to retreat, and Saddam himself ordered a retreat.

The war went on for two years. This was not going as planned. When Iran started getting the upper hand and put Iraq on the defensive, Saddam offered a cease-fire. Khomeini demanded that Hussein resign and pay compensation. Saddam declined, and so the war continued.

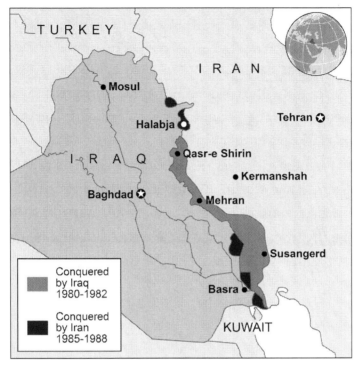

Figure 56. Map of Iran-Iraq War

July 13, 1982: Iran launched Operation Ramadan, an attack to capture Iraq's only port, Basra, and destroy any infrastructure in the country they encountered. Iraq was financing the war through oil sales, through Kuwait and Saudi Arabia. Iran had eyes on the oil to cripple Iraq's ability to make money. Iran attacked any civilian oil shipments of any nation that did business with Iraq in direct defiance of international law. Attacking civilian transport is a war crime.

Before then, it was a regional conflict. As soon as Iran started attacking foreign civilians and messing with the oil supply, the United States, Britain, France, and Germany all got involved and started to back Iraq.

Both sides waged war like it was WWI, digging into a

position, hammering the enemy with artillery, and using chemical weapons.

1988: A war that was supposed to end quickly was in its eighth year. No one was making any progress. Iran had exhausted itself. They couldn't keep throwing away lives to Scud missiles sent at them by Iraq.

Iraq counter-attacked. Khomeini requested a ceasefire six years after he had declined Hussein's attempts. They worked out a peace agreement. After all was done, both sides declared victory, more than a million people were dead, and neither had gained anything from the conflict.

7.1.2 GULF WAR

Iraq's economy and oil infrastructure were wiped out. They owed a ton of money, particularly to Kuwait, who was their next-door oil competitor. Hussein was particularly furious when Kuwait started drilling for oil just over the border in Iraqi territory.

Figure 57. US President George H. W. Bush

President George H. W. Bush (the father of the President who would lead the beginning of the War on Terror) suggested that Kuwait should pay Iraq 10 billion dollars for trespassing and stealing oil. Emir of Kuwait paid nine billion. This annoyed Saddam more.

In 1990, Saddam concocted some excuse that he had a historical claim to the entire country of Kuwait. Iraq invaded and conquered the country in just two days (Figure 58).

Kuwait's leader, Emir Jaber Al-Ahmad Al-Sabah, escaped and fled to Saudi Arabia, along with hundreds of refugees.

Figure 58. Invasion of Kuwait

Al-Sabah spoke to the international community. The UN denounced Saddam and placed sanctions on his country. Hussein declared Kuwait to be the new 19th province of Iraq and started moving soldiers to the border with Saudi Arabia, making everyone very nervous that he was planning another invasion there.

As it happened, Saudi Arabia had been a long ally of the United States. Once again, the United States, Britain, France, and, this time, Australia became involved. They started mobilizing against Iraq on the border in Saudi Arabia in Operation Desert Shield.

Saddam understood what was coming. He declared jihad against the West, despite being secular, and also added the words *Allahu Akbar*, meaning "God is the greatest," onto the

Iraqi flag. Bush organized a massive Coalition of 39 countries to fight Iraq. Saddam got a couple of small dictatorships to pledge support, but only Sudan showed up to the fight. Iraq did not have many friends left under Saddam Hussein's tenure.

November 29, 1990: The UN authorized the use of all necessary force against Iraq if the President did not immediately withdraw from Kuwait by mid-January 1991. Saddam was not a man who liked to back down from a fight.

Figure 59. Operation Desert Storm

Failing to comply, America led a massive air offensive against Iraq. The defensive operation went on the offense. Desert Shield became Operation Desert Storm. Iraq never had a chance. A little over a month later, Iraq's defenses were completely wiped out, losing most of the tanks, artillery, and air force. Operation Desert Saber pushed the Iraqi army back into Iraq. On their way out, Iraq used a scorched earth strategy and set fire to every oil production facility they abandoned.

George H. W. Bush decided not to invade Iraq and depose Saddam, concerned that the country's history of instability would mean that there would be another civil conflict without Hussein. The country would be split into combative warlords. Pay close attention to this part because it will be very important later when his son, George W. Bush, also serves as President.

One of the ceasefire terms required Iraq to hand over any weapons of mass destruction, whether chemical, biological, or nuclear. Saddam was never compliant with weapons inspectors, consistently belligerent and kicking them out while simultaneously claiming he had nothing to hide.

Over the next decade, the US used its cold war strategy and encouraged the Kurds and Shiites to rise and topple Saddam, who had led his country to ruin. Nearly a decade of war with no benefit, followed by sanctions, left the country deeply poor. The terrible state of Iraq inspired two coup attempts, both of which failed in 1992 and 1993. If Saddam was good at anything, he was good at fending off uprisings and coups.

7.1.3 MILITARY ORGANIZATION

Saddam's most significant criterion for military rank was loyalty. He divided his military into three major groups based on how much he trusted them. The regular army, the Republican Guard, and the Special Republican Guard (SRG) (Figure 60). None of the three groups were allowed to talk to each other and never allowed to coordinate military operations.

Figure 60. Special Republican Guard (SRG)

SRG, the most trusted of the groups, was the only group allowed to occupy the capital. Other soldiers not in the SRG weren't even allowed to have maps of Baghdad. Having a map of the city could be part of a plan to attack the capital. Any discussion between the three militaries was a severe offense and could mean execution. The leaders of the three groups had never even met or spoken to each other. They are all supposed to be on the same team, but Saddam made sure they were completely cut off. If one of them tried a coup, Saddam would have the other two get rid of them. This works great to stop coups, but it is a terrible way to fight a war from outside the country.

Soldiers had unrealistic confidence in battle, most of them living their entire lives under the Hussein presidency and spending their childhood growing up being taught that Saddam was great by the television. They also believed that the US was weak, cowardly, and would fold under pressure.

Saddam's paranoia would be a major factor in his downfall. This information will be essential later during the invasion.

7.1.4 IRAQ'S DIVISIONS

The French and British empires divided up the country based on their best guess of what they believed would work and also on how they thought it would be strategically to their advantage. Normally, countries have a basis for what makes their country "them." They have a shared culture or history, a common heritage, or a common religion. In multi-ethnic countries like America and England, this is especially important. People need a reason to look at their neighbors and think of them as countrymen. People need a reason to be on the same team.

Iraq didn't have that glue that holds other countries together.

For one, you have the conflict between the Sunni and Shia Muslims. Their split came about 1,500 years ago, immediately after the death of the prophet Muhammad. The prophet had left no instructions before his death about who would lead his new religion after he died. The Sunni believed that leadership should be passed to the religious leaders who were most qualified. The Shia believed that the succession should pass to the relatives of Muhammad, like a monarchy. Since then, they have separated theologically and culturally as well.

Shia Islam is the majority's in Iran and Iraq, but in most of the world, they are a religious minority.

Eighty percent of Iraq is Arab, but there is also a sizeable ethnic minority, the Kurds, who are spread over several countries, including the north of Iraq. They have their own culture and language but have no homeland of their own. Many of them want to establish their own new country, Kurdistan.

While they are majority Sunni, they had been fiercely abused by Saddam, and many were murdered in a gas attack during the Iran-Iraq War.

TV Mini Series

House of Saddam (2008)

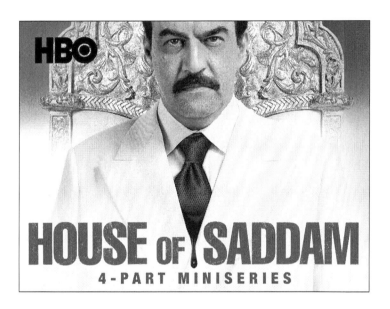

The story of the rise and fall of Saddam Hussein through a mini-series that discovers the inner mechanisms of Saddam Hussein's family and his relationship with his closest consultants.

Directed by: Alex Holmes and Jim O'Hanlon

Starring: Yigal Naor, Shohreh Aghdashloo, Philip Arditti, Amr Waked, Said Taghmaoui, and Christine Stephen-Daly

Book

Playing Atari with Saddam Hussein: Based on a True Story by Ali Fadhil and Jennifer Roy

In early 1991, eleven-year-old Ali Fadhil was fascinated by football, video games, and American television shows. On January 17, 1991, Saddam Hussein, Iraq's dictator, went to war with a coalition commanded by the United States.

In the following days, Ali and his family survived food shortages, bombings, and constant terror. Ali and his brothers played football on the deserted streets of their Basra neighborhood, wondering when or if their father would return from the war front. Cinematic, accessible, and timely, this is the story of one ordinary kid's view of life during the war.

8. IRAQ WAR

After 9/11, Hussein made a terrible error. He publicly applauded the attacks against America, openly happy that someone had attacked his enemy. That may have factored into George W. Bush's decision to classify Iraq as being part of what he called "The Axis of Evil," a trinity of three countries that were not allied with each other: Iran, Iraq, and North Korea.

The US accused Hussein's regime of developing weapons of mass destruction (WMD). This included chemical, biological, and potentially nuclear weapons. The White House showed congress and the UN images of aerial photography and illustrations of weapons manufacturing. A lot of this information came from the man we now know was lying, "Codename: Curveball." The Bush administration also flirted with the idea that Saddam Hussein was connected to Al-Qaeda. They didn't say it, but they implied it frequently. Many Americans, still feeling sore from the attacks, were quick to connect the two.

Both parties in Congress were quick to support the war. The country was divided on the issue. Many people were onboard, while others organized protests and were against it.

Unlike the invasion of Afghanistan, this was a much less popular war for the international community and the Americans. The White House made a case that intelligence showed Iraq was producing nonconventional chemical weapons and had ties to Al-Qaeda.

The US had already made up its mind. Bush had decided to go in with or without the approval of the UN. While diplomats were debating the invasion at the UN, the CIA was already in Iraq gathering intelligence and beginning the planning of the invasion.

Saddam Hussein was prone to blustering, chest-puffing, and acting bigger than he was. If he felt threatened, he always pushed back. But this time, the US wasn't going to wait for UN weapons inspectors to be kicked out again. Unlike the UN, the US was not at all playing around.

Saddam had another problem. He had always ruled his country through fear. He controlled one of the strongest militaries in the region. Whether or not he had WMDs, he needed everyone to believe he had them. If he didn't have the weapons, he could be vulnerable to insurrection from his people or attacks from his neighbors, who universally hated him. However, if he did have WMDs, he would be invaded by America's new Coalition.

Bush organized what he called The Coalition of the Willing. These were countries that agreed to assist the US but not through any treaty. Not all the countries that came along for Afghanistan also came along for this war, notably France, which created some friction between them and the US. The Coalition consisted of 48 countries. Three of those countries contributed troops to the initial invasion force: The United Kingdom, Australia, and Poland. After the invasion was complete, 37 countries that were members of the Coalition also provided some troops.

March 17, 2003: President Bush went on television and gave Saddam a deadline. He and his two sons, Uday and Qusay, needed to leave Iraq or to surrender within 48 hours or face the consequences (Figure 61).

Forty-eight hours later, Saddam Hussein ignored Bush's warnings. Twenty minutes after he failed to meet the deadline, Coalition forces attacked.

Figure 61. US President George W. Bush addresses the nation on Iraq, March 17, 2003

Pre-invasion Planning

On the night before the invasion, Saddam Hussein completed his fourth fiction novel, titled Begone, Demons.

The CIA reached out to the Kurdish Peshmergas, which means "those who face death." These are guerrillas from Kurdistan who were deeply hateful of Saddam after the war crimes Saddam committed against them in the Iran-Iraq war. Saddam had used gas weapons against them and killed over a hundred civilians. Kurdish allies coordinated with the CIA and developed a list of Ba'athist leadership to target.

This information would be very important later on. The majority of the Iraqi military leadership was immediately targeted with airstrikes, leaving the Iraqi military with a broken chain of command. The belief was that the majority of the army was not deeply committed to the regime. Without their leadership, the soldiers would not fight.

The Iraqi military was expecting an attack, but Coalition leadership was planning a broad, unconventional strategy that Iraqi generals were not expecting. Instead of capturing urban centers, the Coalition would focus almost entirely on dismantling the Iraqi government by killing or capturing Iraqi leadership.

Al-Qaim Raid

Intelligence suspected that Iraq had a chemical weapon production site hidden inside of a water treatment facility. Two days before the main invasion, a British elite commando group, the Special Air Service (SAS), deployed and attempted to capture the plant. The defense fought harder than expected, and the commando team was forced to withdraw. Concerned that the weapons might be deployed against them or others, the SAS commandos called in an airstrike. The facility was decimated by a long-range ordinance. The facility was completely wiped out, along with any potential evidence that it was a chemical weapons lab.

When this information was revealed, it hurt the Bush administration's case that Iraq had WMDs.

Al-Dora Farms

Coalition intelligence suspected that they knew the location of Saddam Hussein and his sons. They were believed to be just outside Baghdad, at Al-Dora Farms. There was believed to be a bunker hidden in the farming community. The Coalition sent two F-117 stealth fighters (Figure 62) who dropped bunker-busting bombs on the site. The location was utterly destroyed, and several civilians were killed or wounded. Later, the CIA learned in interrogations with Saddam's secretary; the Husseins were not at that location. Saddam had not been to the area in a decade. The town was destroyed, and people died for nothing.

Just like the Al-Qaim raid, this reinforced the international community's skepticism of the war.

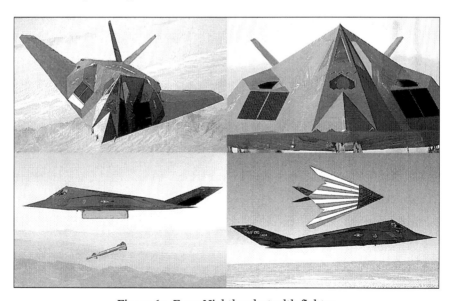

Figure 62. F-117 Nighthawk stealth fighter

The Main Invasion Begins

Figure 63. US aerial bombardment of Baghdad

Traditionally, a country could expect a long period of aerial bombardment (Figure 63) before the main invasion, usually targeting major cities. Once those big cities are weakened, the main invasion force rolls in and occupies the city. Coalition forces did something different. They avoided cities and headed straight for precise targets of the Iraqi leadership, moving and bombing at the same time. They called this tactic "Shock and Awe" because it was designed with the belief that if the leadership was destroyed, the rank-and-file soldiers would surrender or flee. The Coalition remembered from the previous wars with Iraq that the military was dysfunctional and could be broken.

It was also assumed that the majority of the civilian population would welcome the Coalition as liberators who would free them from Saddam. With the tyrant gone, the majority of Iraqis would be thankful and willing to support the Coalition.

Turkey was not supportive of the invasion and refused Coalition forces to invade from inside their borders. The Coalition had to go through Kuwait instead.

Figure 64. Oil well fires in Kuwait

March 19, 2003: Under cover of night, the 160th airborne, known as the "Night Stalkers," destroyed 70 outposts on the southern and western borders. Simultaneously, they launched an amphibious assault on the Al-Faw peninsula. They went straight for the oil infrastructure to capture it. Remember, Iraq was dependent on selling oil. Without oil, they would go broke very quickly. They assaulted the off-shore oil platforms with commandos to take them before they could be sabotaged. The

Coalition already learned from the Gulf War that the Iraqi military would rather destroy oil production than let it fall into enemy hands. Saddam was prone to petty revenge, even at great cost to himself and the people of Iraq.

The teams were able to take the oil platforms and the oil fields on the peninsula. Had they failed at their mission, the Iraqi forces would surely have lit them on fire as they did in Kuwait 10 years earlier (Figure 64). Setting fire to that many oil wells would be an ecological disaster. Coalition forces suffered few casualties.

Nasiriyah

On March 23, the 3rd US infantry maintenance convoy made a wrong turn into Nasiriyah, the Headquarters of Iraqi's 3rd corps. The Iraqi forces hastily prepared an ambush, surprised by the sudden approach of Coalition troops. The US infantry didn't know what hit them. Fifteen of the 18 vehicles were destroyed, and 18 US soldiers were killed or captured.

Later that day, backup arrived. The 2nd marine division stormed the city. They took serious casualties but made a lot of progress in the dense urban environment. During this engagement, six marines died in a friendly fire incident when an A-10 Warthog (Figure 65) mistook their amphibious vehicle for an enemy. The first engagement in Nasiriyah was a disaster.

The next day, Fedayeen Saddam entered the fight.

Fedayeen means, "Those who sacrifice themselves." Fedayeen Saddam were those who sacrificed themselves for Saddam. They were supposed to represent the elite forces of the Ba'athist party, but they weren't trained or better equipped than other troops. Their unique value to the regime was their loyalty. Fedayeen Saddam wore special helmets that were designed to look like Darth Vader's helmet from the Star Wars movies. Saddam's son, Uday, was a huge Star Wars fan and insisted on it.

Figure 65. A-10 Thunderbolt II "Warthog"

Uday Hussein thought it was a great idea to dress his soldiers up like a science fiction movie villain. In reality, Fedayeen Saddam was Uday's private goon squad, not much more than gangsters. When the Fedayeen Saddam weren't fighting Coalition forces, they went into towns and villages, demanding people join in the fighting. They executed anyone who refused.

Fedayeen joined the Iraqi forces. They climbed into ordinary civilian cars, wore civilian clothing, and drove towards Coalition troops waving a white flag, indicating that they were surrendering and wouldn't attack. The insurgents stopped, got out of their car, and approached the Marines. The Marines were hesitant. They knew it could be challenging to know who could be trusted.

Fedayeen then attacked, along with other regular Iraqi forces. They tried using the false surrender as a sneak attack. This is a war crime under the Geneva Convention. They used small arms, assault rifles, and rocket-propelled grenades (RPGs) (Figure 66), which are essentially light, hand-held rocket launchers.

Figure 66. Rocket-propelled grenades (RPGs)

Fifty Marines were wounded, and one vehicle was destroyed. Despite their deception, the Iraqi forces lost the fight. Marines were able to capture the river on the far side of the city, Saddam Canal. The Marines held their ground against counterattacks by the Fedayeen Saddam Militia, who were devoted but unskilled and poorly equipped.

Najaf

To the north of Nasiriyah was Najaf, a city with major roads leading to the crucial cities of Karbala and Baghdad. While the Coalition strategy was to go around major cities and target Iraqi leadership, Najaf was an important exception. Whoever controlled Najaf controlled the roads that cut through the center of Iraq. This city could not be ignored.

Figure 67. Al Kifl and Abu Sukhayr Bridges

The Coalition needed to capture two bridges: one to the north, Al Kifl Bridge, and one to the south, the Abu Sukhayr Bridge (Figure 67). Taking bridges is very difficult. While standing on a bridge, you are a sitting duck. There is very little cover, and there is a narrow channel. Any weapons fired down the bridge are almost guaranteed to hit something. A destroyed vehicle on the bridge can stop all movement until it is removed.

Trying to skip the bridge and cross the river has the same problems. While crossing the water, you have even less cover, you have to fight against a water current, and you are slowed down. You can't take any vehicles with you unless they can be in the water.

To take a bridge, you have to fight from the opposite banks of the river. This can take a long time because you can't maneuver around your enemy.

Codename: Objective Jenkins

The 1st Brigade Combat Team attacked the north bridge on March 25 but made little progress until they were reinforced before dawn. At the same time, Coalition forces had to fight back Iraqi combat engineers who attempted to place explosives on the bridge to destroy it before US forces could take it.

Ultimately, the US was able to cross the bridge and enter Najaf.

Codename: Objective Floyd

At the same time, US forces advanced on the south bridge. Before even reaching the bridge, they made contact with strong resistance from regular and militia forces. One Iraqi soldier drove a full-size city bus and crashed it into a Bradley Fighting Vehicle at full speed. They were eventually able to beat back the Iraqi resistance and cross the bridge into the city.

Taking the City

Najaf was encircled and the bridges captured on March 26, and the fighting forces were relieved by the 101st Airborne. Now, these fresh soldiers had to take the city. Over the next few days, the Airborne Division moved through the town with tanks and infantry.

The 101st deliberately left one road open and unoccupied. They hoped that an open road might bait Iraqi forces to try to move or escape on it.

April 1: After days of intense, close-quarters combat, some Iraqi soldiers took the bait and moved on that suspiciously empty road. They were surprised to be attacked by Coalition snipers who were waiting to ambush them. Helicopter gunships came in and made short work of them.

April 4: After more than a week of fighting, the Coalition officially captured the city.

Basra

To the southeast, British forces faced more resistance than expected in the city of Basra, near the Kuwaiti border. Basra was close to a port with access to the Persian Gulf. Like Najaf, Basra couldn't be ignored. Access to supplies from the sea is crucial to keep soldiers fed and armed with ammunition.

March 27: Basra was well-defended and dug in. It took two weeks of fighting to finally break the garrison. The British lost 11 soldiers. Iraqis suffered casualties estimated as high as 400 to 500.

As tanks rolled through the city, they were greeted by the smiling faces of the locals who cheered and were grateful for defeating Saddam's forces. However, as the crowds gathered, many of them started looting. The happy masses became a mob, running through the streets and taking whatever they could.

Karbala Gap

The Karbala Gap is a 25-mile strip of land between the Euphrates River and Lake Razazah. The Iraqi military was aware of the strategic importance of this location and defended it with two divisions of the Iraqi Army's elite Republican Guard.

What the Iraqi forces did not know was that the Coalition had been feeding false information to the Iraqi military to convince them that the US 4th Infantry Division would be attacking from Turkey in the north. Of course, this wasn't possible because Turkey was not allowing Coalition forces into their land.

The forces in Karbala Gap were led by Saddam's son, Qusay Hussein. He believed that the approaching Coalition forces were a feint, a fake attack and that this was all a ruse to lure him away from protecting Baghdad. He took half of his forces north, away from Karbala Gap. This meant that half the forces were on a mission to waste their time, while Karbala was left half as strong.

April 1: Ironically, on April Fool's Day, Lieutenant General Raad Al-Hamdani warned that if Qusay didn't go back to Karbala and reinforce the Republican Guard, Baghdad had no chance. Qusay should have listened to him, but he didn't. That very day, the Coalition took Karbala and the city of Musayyib.

Two days later, Qusay tried to undo his mistake and mobilized a counter-attack. An Iraqi armored division approached Karbala in the night but was wiped out by aircraft before they could even make their attack (Figure 68).

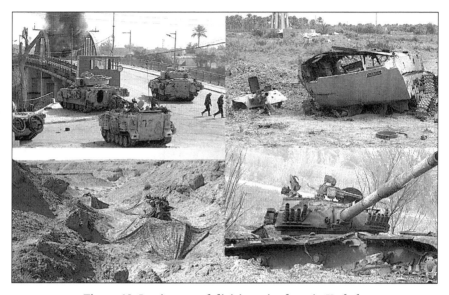

Figure 68. Iraqi armored division wiped out in Karbala

Baghdad

With the key targets secured, it was time to take the capital of Iraq: Baghdad.

By this point, most of the Iraqi military was gone. They lost their leadership in targeted strikes. Soldiers took off their uniforms and tried to blend back into the population. The Shock and Awe strategy was working.

Some Ba'athist militia still tried, perhaps out of loyalty to their party. Or maybe because they were terrified of what would happen to them if they lost the war. In any case, there were still holdouts who wouldn't give up, but they were disorganized and not well supported.

Army Colonel David Perkins led the 2nd Brigade, 3rd Infantry Division, and they attempted what he called a "Thunder Run," driving a column of tanks straight through the city. They were attacked by militia wearing civilian clothing, attacking from windows and rooftops with RPGs and small arms fire. The column was in a very vulnerable position and executed a fighting withdrawal.

Marines stormed the Diyala Bridge on the eastern side of the city and moved along the bank of the Euphrates River. They were fearful of vehicle attacks, suicide bombers, and militia pretending to be civilians. Coalition soldiers were nervous about any non-military they saw. There was no way to tell if they were friendly or an enemy. On the banks of the river, Marines fired on any car that refused to stop when ordered.

April 7: Colonel Perkins attempted another Thunder Run. This time he was successful and rolled through the city at a lightning pace, speeding towards critical locations in the city. The Colonel spent that night sleeping in Saddam's palace.

April 9: The Coalition declares victory. Baghdad is captured. The civilians are enthusiastic and begin tearing down statues of Saddam (Figure 69). There was a celebration in the streets. But, just like in Basra, the jubilation quickly turned for the worst and became massive looting as the crowds began ransacking buildings and shops and taking what they pleased. It didn't end until the Coalition military asserted themselves and acted as the new police in the suddenly lawless city.

Figure 69. Civilians tearing down statues of Saddam

Saddam Hussein wasn't found. The Coalition continued searching for him and any other high-ranking people who escaped.

The Iraqi people were shocked by the invasion. They didn't believe it would happen until the moment it did. That includes Saddam Hussein, who was accustomed to being threatened. He assumed the Coalition couldn't pull it off, remembering Vietnam and Black Hawk Down, the incident in Mogadishu.

8.1 A NEW DEMOCRACY

Figure 70. President Bush on the USS Abe Lincoln, wearing a flight suit and in front of a banner declaring "mission accomplished."

May 1, 2003: President Bush on the USS Abe Lincoln, wearing a flight suit, announced the end of combat operations in front of a banner declaring "mission accomplished."

The invasion was the easy part. For the next eight years, Coalition forces would remain in the area for a counter-insurgency. The mission was accomplished. But just like in Afghanistan, there was a new mission: to build a new nation.

The Coalition organized a new provisional government, like training wheels for democracy. This was the starting place for some appearance of organization until they could create a real constitution and government. There were problems with this approach right away. The internal politics of Iraq were more complicated and turbulent than the White House had anticipated.

When the new governing council was publicized, there were 13 Shia and 10 Sunni, five of whom were Kurdish. Many Sunnis were not happy about this. From the Western perspective, those numbers seemed fair because they were representative of the population. From the Sunni perspective, it looked like the Shia would be in control from now on. Remember, the Sunni had the power before. With a Shia majority government, they were concerned about payback. They wondered if maybe Saddam was right not to trust the West. Sunni concerns were not unreasonable. Shiites in the government had many vacancies to fill in jobs that Ba'athists formerly held. The Shia government was replacing all the old jobs with other Shia and taking over the whole government.

8.2 THE INSURGENCY

Despite Saddam's tyranny, many Iraqis did not like America. Their only contact with the US before the Iraq War was occasionally bombing strikes. They also knew about the US attempts to destabilize the country by financing insurrectionist anti-government rebels. Many didn't trust America after the Iran-Iraq War. Remember, the US was friendly to Iraq while it was at war with Iran. But once Iraq invaded Kuwait, the US became their enemy.

Saddam had also spent a ton of money winning the hearts of the religiously devoted. While his spiritual devotion is highly questionable, he certainly wasn't above pretending to be a devout Muslim to manipulate people. He built lots of mosques and was always working hard to project the image that he was devout.

Even those who hated Saddam and were glad to see him gone weren't necessarily friendlier to the US, whom many were suspicious of, remembering the recent colonial era where foreign Western powers controlled the Middle East from afar.

Very importantly, the US failed to anticipate the importance of the major religious divide in Iraq between the two major groups: the Sunni and the Shia.

The Ba'athists were a Sunni party, but the majority of Iraqis are Shiite. Their adversarial neighbor Iran was a Shia country. Ba'athists brutally repressed the Shia, fearing that they could be used by Iran to overthrow them. If they caught the faintest whiff of rebellion, the Ba'ath party responded with group punishment and mass executions.

The Coalition had a good game plan to invade. They didn't have much of a plan for what happened after.

Shia militia began looking to take vengeance against the Sunni, blaming them for Saddam's oppression. With the military destroyed and the police nowhere to be found, these two religious sects started fighting against each other. The state was in anarchy; the provisional government was unable to do anything about it. A sectarian civil war was coming.

Coalition forces remained in the area to act as the de facto police and perform a counter-terror and counter-insurgency role.

2004: US forces raided a mosque run by an Imam who was preaching against America and taught would-be insurgents how to make bombs. Weapons and bombs were found inside the mosque, but while searching the place, the soldiers wrecked the mosque and disrespected the temple. This was considered a profoundly offensive act to many Muslims, not because a bomb-maker was arrested but because a mosque was desecrated in the process. Extremist religious leaders called upon the faithful to punish those who did this, claiming that they were here to attack Islam, not just Saddam.

Because militia and terror groups attacked Coalition forces while wearing civilian clothes, the Coalition had no choice but to be suspicious of everyone in civilian clothes. Anyone could be a potential attacker. Innocent Iraqis did not like being treated like they were terrorists when they were innocent. This created a powerful mutual distrust between Iraqis and Coalition soldiers.

The CIA rounded up the former spies in Iraq. Instead of punishing them for murder and torture, the CIA gave them their old jobs back. One thing you can say about Saddam is that he was good at stopping terrorists. It was not a problem in his country, even when many of his neighbors had constant terrorist attacks. The Iraqi spies were an important reason why. Since the Coalition was there to defeat terrorism, the CIA weighed their options and decided their best option was to let these spies continue working the way they had before.

Battles erupted between Shia and Sunni neighborhoods. Violence and chaos consumed Iraq. The Coalition's inability to understand Iraqi culture and politics turned the country upside down. By 2006, the country was in a full-scale civil war. Both Sunni and Shia groups attempted ethnic cleansings, displacing millions of people.

One major blunder made by the Bush administration was to disband all members of the Sunni-majority army. Coalition governments were worried that they couldn't be trusted in the military. This plan backfired. Instead of integrating them into the new government, they left these men unemployed and under the yolk of a Shiite government. So, Iraq now was filled with men who had no job and also happened to be trained soldiers and who held a major grudge against the new government and Coalition forces. This mistake essentially created a perfect situation for an insurgency.

At the same time, Osama bin Laden's ally, Zarqawi (Figure 71), came to Iraq to participate in the insurgency. Remember, he was a member of Al-Qaeda who fought with Osama bin Laden in Afghanistan. He called his militia the Tawhid wal-Jihad. With America so close, they were within range of Al-Qaeda forces. That group was strengthened by other jihadists from the region, and many of those were former Iraqi soldiers.

They pledged themselves to Osama bin Laden and renamed their group Al-Qaeda in Iraq (AQI).

Figure 71. Abu Musab Al-Zarqawi

The modern military is designed to go to foreign countries and win as quickly as possible. The military isn't designed for the task of policing a nation or creating a new government from scratch. In all military matters, some concepts and strategies are tried and true. There are reliable ways of doing things that have been tested in the laboratory of war. This is called military doctrine. Militaries and branches within the military have their distinct doctrine that evolves as they learn more and as they have to change with the times. There is no established military doctrine for invading a country, removing partisans, providing security, and then leaving the country with people who love you and are thankful to you.

Afghanistan and Iraq became the hot spot for anyone with

a grudge against the United States. People from all over the world who wanted to fight America made their way to Iraq and Afghanistan. These people didn't even necessarily care about Iraq or Afghanistan. They didn't have to care about Saddam Hussein or Al-Qaeda. Instead of just fighting a single force with a common goal, the insurgency was made up of countless people who had their reasons and vendettas. Many of those insurgents had little to nothing in common with each other. But as we've realized time and time again, it's very common in the world for people who don't have any reason to be friends to work together against a common enemy.

8.3 WMDS

Figure 72. Chemical weapons

There is a lot of disagreement still about Iraq's weapons of mass destruction (WMDs). When the Pentagon was making a case for invasion, they claimed that Iraq not only had chemical weapons (Figure 72) but that they were producing more or developing depleted uranium to make what's called a dirty bomb. This is like a bomb that uses radioactive waste but not to create a radioactive nuclear explosion. A dirty bomb explodes like an ordinary bomb, but it is full of radioactive material. The radioactive dust spreads out over a wide area, covering it with extremely dangerous, toxic particles. This dust could make the area essentially unlivable for hundreds if not thousands of years. Trace amounts of this dust in the water supply could cause cancer, birth defects, and diseases that could slowly kill many people.

For the first few years of the war, we were promised that they were hot on the trail of these WMDs. But after President Bush won his second election, it came out that the administration had given up on finding them at all. Those who believed in the WMD story and those who doubted it were both almost right. Chemical weapons were found buried in remote parts of the desert. They had been there for a very long time. However, the CIA's intelligence about the weapons development program was a bust. As you know, the source of this information, "Curveball," was a liar.

It's hard to know at this point how much of the war was based on lies created by the United States government and how much of it was based on lies told to the United States government.

The connection supposedly linking Al-Qaeda to Saddam Hussein could never be verified. Saddam was not a religious fanatic by any means. He ran his country like a gangster. He would have much more in common with a man like Al Capone than with bin Laden. Saddam Hussein was not a fan of religious fundamentalism, although he wasn't above using his peoples' religious faith to manipulate them. He would speak using religious language and project the image that he was a devout Muslim. But he was primarily interested in enriching himself and his family, and spiritual matters didn't motivate him.

8.4 FINDING SADDAM

Saddam's two sons, Uday and Qusay, were killed in the bombing early in the war. Uday was an unstable psychopath, while Qusay was a reliable, trusted ally to his father.

December 13, 2003: Saddam Hussein wasn't found for another eight months after the invasion. He was hiding out in a mud hut in the middle of nowhere, a far lower lifestyle than the luxury and wealth he was accustomed to.

A ranking member of Saddam's security team was captured during a raid. He told interrogators where Saddam was hiding out. A well-armed special forces team cut power in the area and raided the shack. They expected a lot of resistance, but there was none. The shack was empty. Then they found a trap door. Saddam was hiding in a hole in the ground (Figure 73).

October 19, 2005: The dictator was arrested and put on trial for old war crimes before the Iraqi Special Tribunal (Figure 73). He was found guilty of committing genocide against the Kurdish people.

The trial was quite a show. Saddam was defiant in the early stages, refusing to come to court, lashing out and shouting at the judge, and questioning the court's legitimacy. During the trial, three of Saddam's defense attorneys were assassinated. The last one was killed by men dressed as police. Whether they were police is unknown.

Saddam went on a hunger strike but gave up after missing one meal. He accused his captors of torturing him. The judge excused himself from the case at one point, and a new judge was put in, alleging government interference.

December 30, 2006: Saddam Hussein was executed by hanging. But even with him gone, the Iraqi people were suffering under a new form of terror.

Figure 73. Saddam arrested and put on trial for old war crimes

YouTube

During the invasion, Mohammed Saeed Al-Sahhaf, the Iraqi Information Minister, nicknamed "Baghdad Bob," told increasingly silly lies on Iraqi TV that Iraq was winning the war. At about the 5-minute mark of the video provided by Alex Jones, Al-Sahhaf claims that Coalition troops were committing suicide en masse.

Watch it here: https://youtu.be/94VhPH7BouY

More of his lies could be watched here on YouTube: https://youtu.be/iF_D9ILqmQo

TV Mini Series

Generation Kill (2008)

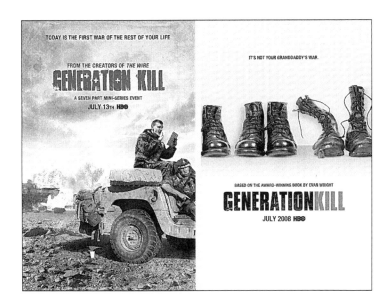

Based on the award-winning book of the same title by Evan Wright, this mini series is exceptionally realistic—so realistic that some of the "actors" are not actors. They are the actual Marines, playing themselves, who lived the events portrayed in the show.

Directed by: Susanna White and Simon Cellan Jones

Starring: Alexander Skarsgård, James Ransone, Lee Tergesen, Jon Huertas, Stark Sands, Billy Lush, Jonah Lotan, Wilson Bethel, and Marc Menchaca

9. OPERATION INHERENT RESOLVE

While Iraq was weak and fighting itself, a new player entered the stage. The religiously fanatical militia ISIS conquered Iraq quickly and formed their short-lived government. ISIS is legendary now for its violence, cruelty, and complete disregard for human rights and dignity.

ISIS, as it is commonly known, changed its name several times. This can be confusing. When we talk about Al-Qaeda of Iraq (AQI) and ISIS, we are talking about the same terrorist organization (Figure 74).

The Rise of ISIS

Before they were called ISIS (Islamic State of Iraq and Syria), they were called Al-Qaeda in Iraq (AQI).

Despite Al-Qaeda being one of the motivations for invading Iraq, Al-Qaeda was not a significant player in Iraq until after the invasion. AQI didn't show up until after Coalition forces arrived, with the express purpose of attacking foreigners who were now so conveniently close. AQI became one of the major insurgent forces fighting the Coalition.

Initially, AQI had some support from many Sunnis who were angry about the new government and unhappy that Saddam was removed and replaced with a Shia-majority government.

These were religious fundamentalists. In territories they controlled, they banned music they disapproved of. They banned smoking. They created very strict dress codes. Women weren't allowed to show their hair in public.

Figure 74. ISIS

They enforced their new rules with absolute cruel violence. Breaking even small rules could be punished with whipping, cutting off hands, or beheading. ISIS would publicize these punishments. They shot videos of their executions and posted them on the internet. They got a lot of attention in the news for murdering journalists. In one very famous and horrifying video, they lit a man inside a cage on fire. The videos were so horrifying and shocking that drug dealers in Mexico and Central and South America began copying them. The drug cartels saw the terror these videos caused and wanted to do the same thing to their enemies. In 2004, Osama bin Laden saw that AQI was effective and sent his ally Zarqawi to lead Al-Qaeda in Iraq.

By 2006, AQI's brutality lost any support of ordinary

Sunnis. Ordinary Iraqis were not eager to see religious fanatics cutting off people's heads for minor religious violations. They were so concerned about Al-Qaeda that they began to work with US forces against them. AQI was so bad that Sunnis turned on a fellow Sunni organization and made allies with the Americans they hated just a couple of years before.

Even the actual Al-Qaeda was not pleased with AQI. They weren't just targeting foreigners for attacks. They were also waging war against Shiites. Al-Qaeda wasn't trying to start an Islamic civil war between Muslims, but Al-Qaeda in Iraq was. Zarqawi was taking the organization in a new direction, contrary to Osama bin Laden's orders. AQI was ambitious. They didn't just want to kick Coalition forces out. They wanted to create a wholly new Islamic State that spanned the region. They changed their name to ISIS.

That same year, Zarqawi, nicknamed "Sheikh of the slaughterers," was killed by a bomb dropped on him from an F-16C. This didn't slow the organization down. They allied with Ba'athists who hated the Western presence and wanted all Coalition forces gone. ISIS and Ba'athists were not obvious allies, but in this war, alliances happen by necessity, not by mutual friendship.

Across the border in Syria, the dictator Assad allowed ISIS to use their borders to move terrorists, weapons, and supplies, to Iraq. This went on from 2006-2009.

The Surge

2007: Coalition forces reached out to Sunni leadership in Iraq and made a deal with them. They built an alliance to fight back against ISIS. They called this strategy "The Awakening."

In addition, Bush ordered an increase in the troop presence, called "The Surge." The military developed a new counterinsurgency policy. The new plan was to win "hearts and minds." The Coalition had to earn the respect and friendship of the people of Iraq. The mission to defeat terrorists couldn't be won if the locals hated the foreign presence.

This meant giving more respect and understanding to religious differences and changed the rules of engagement to minimize civilian casualties. Bombing and explosives were discouraged.

This change in direction was fruitful. Over the next two years, ISIS was effectively pushed out of Iraq by 2009, with ISIS seeking refuge in Syria. They needed time to regroup and plan their next move.

Islamic State (Not) in Iraq

The Shiite Prime Minister of Iraq, Maliki, was doing precisely what the Sunnis worried he would do. Maliki ruled on sectarian lines. He ruled in ways that benefited Shiites at the expense of Sunnis. He was giving essential jobs and positions to only Shia. He was violently cracking down on Sunni protests. He even arrested Sunni politicians with flimsy accusations. He gave money and weapons to Shiite militias.

In 2010, the leadership of ISIS was taken by a man named Abu Bakr Al-Baghdadi. Al-Baghdadi had spent the previous few years in a Coalition prison in Iraq. He used his time there to make contacts with other extremists and develop a network of allies. Some were terrorists. Some were former Ba'athists who were imprisoned for political reasons. The correctional officers allowed Al-Baghdadi to move freely around the prison because he was good at resolving disputes and fights between other prisoners. Eventually, he was released from prison because he was considered low-threat. His parole board was very, very wrong.

Al-Baghdadi took the group into a whole new direction, far beyond what even Zarqawi had planned.

In 2011, Bush was no longer president, replaced by Barack Obama. Coalition forces began a withdrawal, as agreed upon between the Bush administration and the Iraqi government. Unfortunately, all the progress made using The Awakening strategy was undone. Iraq was once again swallowed up by violence without the presence of the US military.

ISIS saw an opportunity and returned to Iraq. They tried to market themselves as Sunni heroes to fight against Maliki. They grew their numbers and power, waiting for the right moment to attack.

ISIS attacked Mosul, Iraq's second-largest city. Only 800 ISIS fighters attacked a force of 30,000 Iraqi troops. The overwhelmingly large army dropped their weapons and ran away immediately. Mosul was a predominantly Sunni city, including the soldiers defending it. They were unwilling to fight and die fighting other Sunnis to protect a Shiite Prime Minister who was unkind to Sunni.

ISIS had sights on Baghdad and much bigger plans than just defeating Maliki. ISIS wanted to create a total theocracy in the region. They wanted to conquer Iraq and Syria and merge them into a new state governed by medieval interpretations of Islamic doctrine.

Sunnis were stuck between a rock and a hard place. On the one hand, they had Maliki and Shiites oppressing them. On the other, they had a terrorist militia group that would execute them for being too modern.

ISIS Terror Operations

While ISIS was conquering Syria and Iraq, they were also conducting terror operations abroad. These are a few, but this is far from a complete list.

San Bernardino

December 2, 2015: A husband and wife opened fire with rifles at the Inland Regional Center in San Bernardino, California (Figure 75). They killed 14 and injured 17 others, making it one of the deadliest mass shootings in American history.

ISIS did not direct this attack. The married couple were not in contact with ISIS. The wife had pledged allegiance to ISIS and Al-Baghdadi on social media just before they went on their murder spree.

A Couple Opened Fire With Rifles

The SUV Involved In The **San Bernardino** Shooting

Figure 75. A couple opened fire with rifles and the SUV involved in the San Bernardino Shooting

ISIS often relied on "lone wolves," people who aren't organized or directed. Entirely on their own, they plan to perform an act of terror on behalf of another organization. Another name for this is "stochastic terrorism," when a terror group encourages people using propaganda to become "lone wolves" and commit terror acts on their own.

Paris Attacks

November 13, 2015: Nine men split into three-person groups, strapped on suicide vests, and brought rifles to the crowded streets of Paris on a busy Friday night. The nine men shot and blew up as many people as they could before being killed. They murdered 129 people and wounded hundreds of others. Seven of them died during their attack. Two were found and killed a few days later by police.

ISIS claimed responsibility for the attack soon after.

Figure 76. Paris attacks

Russian Plane Tragedy

October 31, 2015: A Russian airliner crashed in the Sinai Peninsula. Every passenger was killed, a total of 224 people. Russian investigators found traces of explosives in the debris. Soon after, ISIS claimed responsibility.

Charlie Hebdo

January 7, 2015: Three Islamic militants with AK-47s attacked the office of the satirical paper, Charlie Hebdo. They killed 12 people, eight of whom were cartoonists. A few days later, authorities found a video of one of the gunmen pledging allegiance to ISIS. Strangely, the two other gunmen had declared their loyalty to Al-Qaeda, which was no longer affiliated with ISIS.

Tunisia Beach Resort

June 26, 2015: At a Tunisian beach resort, a man dressed as a tourist opened up his umbrella to reveal an AK-47 rifle. He fired at European sunbathers. He murdered 39 people, most of whom were tourists. ISIS claimed responsibility the next day. It remains one of the deadliest attacks in Tunisia's history.

The Fall of ISIS

At the height of their success, ISIS controlled one-third of Iraq and large portions of Syria. They set up their government and collected taxes, and imposed their laws. Their militia worked like police, and their court system was based on fringe interpretations of Islamic law.

ISIS needed to hold land and act as a legitimate government for long enough to finally be accepted as a real country. Holding territory was their strategy to be recognized instead of dismissed as a mere terror group.

The operation to take down ISIS was called Operation Inherent Resolve. It was formally announced in 2014 and continues to this day. So long as ISIS exists, so does Inherent Resolve.

Second Battle of Tikrit

Iraqi forces had tried and failed to retake the city of Tikrit in 2014, now a major ISIS stronghold.

Iraqi forces teamed up with Shiite militias supported by Iran, and several Iranian officers, despite Iran being the former enemy of Iraq. Thirty thousand men showed up to fight ISIS and push them out of the city. They encircled Tikrit, cutting off ISIS's access to external supplies or reinforcements, and leaving them nowhere to flee. This would be a true test if Iraq were capable of defeating ISIS.

Forces took Al-Dur first, a town just outside of Tikrit. US airpower bombarded the city, leaving much of it in ruin. Then Iraqi ground forces moved in from the north and south of the city simultaneously, pushing ISIS forces to the center of the city.

ISIS slowed Iraqi advances by laying mines, booby traps, and using car bombs.

After losing Tikrit, ISIS retaliated by ambushing unarmed cadets at Camp Speicher, a nearby Iraqi Air Force training location. They executed well over a thousand cadets, all of whom were Shia and non-Muslim. This massacre is considered the second deadliest terrorist attack in world history, with 9/11 being the first most deadly.

Third Battle of Fallujah

February 26, 2016: Fallujah was the first city that ISIS conquered in Iraq. The Iraqi army surrounded the city. It asked anyone who could leave the area to do so before the fighting. Anyone who couldn't leave was asked by the Iraqi army to hang white flags in their windows to show that they weren't a threat. ISIS forbade anyone within the city from leaving. Anyone caught trying to escape before the battle was punished severely.

Figure 77. Third Battle of Fallujah

May 22: Code-named Operation Breaking Terrorism, the mission to recapture Fallujah began. Iraqi military met stiff resistance immediately. During the initial fighting, 3,000 citizens of Fallujah successfully fled the city.

June 1: Many had already fled. ISIS began rounding up civilians and forcing them to move to the center of the city. They knew that the Iraqi military would be hesitant to fire on an area with a dense civilian population. Essentially, ISIS used the city's people as human shields.

June 3: As Iraqi forces began their slow advance into the city, they received word from another military in nearby Saqlawiyah. They had found a tunnel that was about three and a half miles long, and it led to Fallujah. ISIS had been sneaking in reinforcements and supplies through the underground tunnel. The forces in Saqlawiyah demolished the tunnel, cutting off all outside help to ISIS.

June 12: A total of 40,000 people have fled the city. ISIS had lost control of the population.

June 13: Among the people fleeing, militants are caught hiding among them wearing civilian clothes, abandoning the battle. ISIS's ranks are losing confidence.

June 16: Iraqi military leadership reported that ISIS is broken. They began to try to escape the city. They weren't just retreating. They were abandoning ISIS.

June 26: Iraqi forces recaptured the city of Fallujah and stamped out other pockets of nearby resistance over the next two days. Three thousand ISIS militants were dead, and 2,000 more surrendered. The Iraqi military lost an unknown number but estimated about only 300.

Battle of Mosul

This battle was for the second-largest city in Iraq, with 1.5 million people living there, and it had oil. This was a crucial city for ISIS to control, and they wouldn't give up easily. If they lost the city, it could send the message that the Islamic State wasn't ordained by God, and the ISIS militants would lose faith in their cause.

It was a fierce and lengthy battle of attrition that lasted for more than nine months.

October 16, 2016: Codename Operation "We Are Coming, Nineveh" was the plan to retake Mosul. This was a joint operation between the Coalition, Peshmerga, and Iraqi forces. The Peshmerga began by clearing out any ISIS forces in the nearby area.

Figure 78. Battle of Mosul

October 18: The Iraqi army began clearing out the neighboring villages before they took the city. Locals began rebelling against ISIS and fighting them or disobeying and fleeing from them. ISIS had to spend as much time quelling the rebellion as they did fight off the army.

October 20: ISIS deliberately set fire to a sulfur processing plant, killing two people from the gas and injuring over a thousand who were close enough to inhale the fumes.

November 1: The surrounding areas had been cleansed of ISIS. Iraqi special forces entered the city from the east. ISIS stacked tires and set them on fire, filling the city with a putrid, black smoke that interfered with visibility. The battles in the surrounding regions had moved quickly, but progress slowed when they began the major offensive. Hundreds of thousands of civilians fled the city, creating a massive humanitarian crisis. The city was torn apart.

Over the next few months, Iraqi forces endured sniper fire, suicide bombers, and mortar attacks.

Iraqi forces destroyed several bridges leading into the city, cutting off any escape routes for ISIS and any way to get outside help.

Iraqi progress moved slowly. The ISIS strategy of using sneak attacks required the army to advance slowly and carefully. As they moved in, they encountered car bombs and homes rigged with explosives and other booby traps.

ISIS was eventually wiped out. What remained of them fled and were chased back towards Syria.

July 9, 2017: The President of Iraq declared that Mosul had been liberated.

Raqqa Campaign

Meanwhile, Syria was trying to liberate its city, Raqqa. This was the city that ISIS declared as its capital and where Al-Baghdadi declared himself the Caliph—the Islamic ruler—of his new empire. This was a symbolically crucial location. If the capital could be taken, ISIS was finished. This battle was long and bloody. Both Syria and ISIS had everything on the line.

The Coalition joined with Democratic anti-Assad Syrian militants, Kurdish forces, and Turkey to destroy ISIS once and for all.

November 6, 2016: Operation Wrath of Euphrates began, one of the most complex operations by the Coalition.

ISIS began repurposing downed drones. They used them as scouts to direct suicide truck bombers to find their targets. ISIS filled trucks with large amounts of unexploded ordinance they found in the city. A martyr would then drive the truck at their target and detonate.

Figure 79. Raqqa Campaign

In the complex maze of ruins, ISIS snipers could pick off enemies who weren't careful and pin down positions. The battle was a slow grind. ISIS would not quit. They continued their tactics of using civilians as human shields. They made booby traps, even arming children's toys with explosive devices. If wounded, they would lie in wait for the enemy to approach and then detonate their suicide vests to take others down with them.

During the conflict, the Coalition was extremely distrustful of each other. Syrian forces were concerned about Turkey moving in and taking back territory but keeping it for themselves. At the same time, both were worried about Kurdish forces potentially using the chaos as an opportunity to start their own new country, Kurdistan, using territory previously held by Iraq and Syria. And the Syrian Democrats were still at war with the Assad regime. Getting all of these people to work together was very difficult, and throughout the campaign, they seemed to be competing with each other as much as they were with ISIS.

October 20, 2017: Raqqa was finally liberated. By the end, the city was completely decimated. It was nearly uninhabitable. Buildings were pock-marked with bullet holes or collapsed; the area completely looted of anything valuable. The streets were filled with destroyed vehicles and concrete debris.

The battle took 11 months. Throughout the battle, thousands died on both sides, and 200,000 civilians fled the city, joining the massive refugee crisis that was becoming a global problem. Between Syria and Iraq, an estimated 8 million people had been displaced. Countless fled the area, looking for homes elsewhere, with many escaping to Europe and the Americas.

Even as people try to return to their homes and rebuild, they must be careful of leftover booby traps created by ISIS fighters.

Al-Baghdadi Killed by a Robot and a Dog

Al-Baghdadi has been killed several times. He was declared dead once in 2015. That wasn't true. He was also reported dead in 2017. Again, not true. But the third time was the charm.

October 27, 2019: Delta Force worked alongside Iraqi and Turkish forces to take down the leader of ISIS. They finally found Al-Baghdadi in a compound in northwest Syria. Delta Force arrived in helicopters for a nighttime raid.

Figure 80. Abu Bakr Al-Baghdadi

With his enemies surrounding him, Al-Baghdadi (Figure 80) fled into a network of underground tunnels. He was cornered by a military robot and a dog. With nowhere to run, Al-Baghdadi detonated his suicide vest, killing himself and two children who were also hiding, collapsing the tunnel. The dog was injured but made a full recovery.

His identity was confirmed with DNA tests, and ISIS also confirmed it a few days later.

The Fall of ISIS

The land taken by ISIS was recovered by Syria and Iraq, respectively. Many surviving ISIS members became disillusioned with the group. They were promised heaven on earth and that God was guiding their actions. Instead, they saw nothing but lies, violence, and horror. Many tried returning to their old lives and forgetting what happened. Others left the group and signed on with other militias or terror organizations. The thing about terror groups is that they are often far less secure than you'd expect. Members of these groups often leave and join other groups very easily.

Terrorism hasn't ended, but it has been given a good whupping.

2018: With ISIS gone, violence in Iraq has reduced to its lowest level since 2008. Much of the insurgency disappeared when Al-Qaeda and ISIS were gone. The country isn't stable, and attacks are still happening, but things have cooled down.

Figure 81. US President Donald Trump

2020: The Iraqi parliament voted for all foreign troops to leave the country. This was in violation of the agreement between the US and Iraq to leave a small contingent of troops present. Then, President Trump (Figure 81) refused to remove them, and they remain there to this day, concerned that another ISIS will rise and the US will have to return to Iraq for the third time.

ISIS made promises that it couldn't keep. It promised a paradise for believers, and it promised that God would protect them because they were fighting for God. None of these things were true. Once the truth was exposed, ISIS had no leg to stand on. Their promises brought nothing but death and destruction, and few would ever listen to them again.

TV Series

Black Crows (2017)

A dramatic show about living in ISIS-controlled territory. A major theme is people becoming disillusioned with ISIS and learning that their promises are lies.

Directed by: Adel Adeeb, Hussam Alrantisi, Kinan Iskandarani, Saeed Rayed, and Hussein Shawkat

Starring: Rashed Al Shamrani, Sayed Rajab, and Dina Talaat

Movie

The 15:17 to Paris (2018)

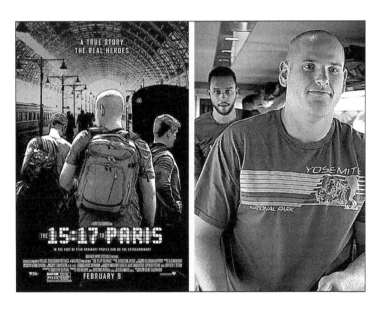

This is about the Paris Train Attack and the Americans who stopped it.

Directed by: Clint Eastwood

Starring: Anthony Sadler, Alek Skarlatos, Spencer Stone, Judy Greer, and Jenna Fischer

10. CONCLUSION

George W. Bush made several mistakes during his presidency. One thing he got right was he always worked very hard to not blame all Muslims for the actions of the most fanatical among them. Bin Laden believed that America was at war with Islam. Bush wanted to make it crystal clear that America was not at war with Islam—America was at war with terrorists. In speeches, he says this over and over again. It wasn't easy to appreciate this at the time, but now it's very clear why.

Osama bin Laden and Al-Qaeda's terrorism was entirely predicated on the belief that the West wanted to launch a new crusade against Islam. Bush was careful never to let America send the message that bin Laden was right.

Terrorism is a tactic. A war on terror is a war against a tactic. One of the terrorist's greatest weapons is propaganda. To defeat terrorists, the Coalition learned that the terrorists had to be starved of things that would be used as propaganda. The greatest recruitment tool that Al-Qaeda had was to find people who hated America. So long as America could make as few enemies as possible, Al-Qaeda's recruitment dried up.

The long-term project in the Middle East and the rest of the world will be to make friends, not enemies. The mission against terrorism cannot be successful if the United States makes more enemies.

Terrorists all have a few features in common:

1- They are always on the losing side of whatever conflict they are in.
2- They believe that humans' strongest motivator is fear.

3- They believe that their cause is so important that it's worth murdering strangers.

You can't win a war on a tactic. There's no end to it. Wherever you find people who are desperate and fanatical for their cause, be it religious or not, you will find a few people who are morally bankrupt enough to murder innocent people.

Terrorism can be fought by:

1- Targeting terrorists and minimizing any harm to innocents.
2- Helping those in need so that they won't become the people that terrorists like to recruit: desperate, angry people who have nothing to lose.
3- Consistently show fearlessness in the face of terror attacks. Prove that fearlessness overcomes fear. Terror cannot work as a tactic if the enemy is fearless.

Men like Saddam Hussein did not have much difficulty with terrorists. His regime was paranoid, brutal, and had no respect for human rights. This gave him a lot of room to fight terrorists. However, if the cost of defeating terrorism is living under the Ba'athist dictatorship, what is gained for the people of Iraq? If the cost of relief from terror is tyranny, is the price worth it?

Saddam Hussein, Osama bin Laden, and Abu Bakr Al-Baghdadi are gone, but the troubles of the Middle East are still there.

The sectarian, nationalistic, ethnic, and tribal divisions in the region haven't been cured.

Kurds are still a large population without a homeland and a complicated relationship with their neighbors.

Syria remains under the control of the dictator Bashar Al-Assad (Figure 82). The democratic army that liberated Raqqa failed to bring democracy to Syria.

Figure 82. Bashar Al-Assad

Divisions between Sunni and Shia haven't been soothed. Old grudges still simmer.

The new Afghan government has failed to control their country, as many before have. The Taliban still lingers there, with less power than before, but always re-emerging like a weed after it's been pulled.

The Taliban is still in Afghanistan. They don't have the power, numbers, and territory they once had, but they are seemingly implacable. President Biden (Figure 83) has announced a complete withdrawal from the region beginning on September 11, 2021.

The Coalition still hasn't learned how to build a new

country from the ground up.

This part of the world is very complex. If you've read through this book, you know more about the War on Terror than most grownups know. In the future, be sure to keep an eye and an ear out for news in this part of the world. Even though it is very far away, it's also very close. What happens there matters to us here.

Figure 83. US President Joe Biden

11. ABOUT THE AUTHOR

Ryan Rhoderick is a seasoned high school history teacher and author of the Greatest Battles for Boys book series, including The War on Terror.

As an educator and a father, he realized that boys lagged behind girls in reading. After sifting through dozens of studies about the growing gap between boys and girls, he decided to write a series of action-packed history books for his son. These books were easy to read and written to pique his son's interest and draw him away from his first-person shooter video games.

Ryan's son and subsequently his friends devoured the series and asked for more. It's then when Ryan decided to publish these books for all boys.

If your son is infatuated with video games and action figures, he will definitely love the Greatest Battles for Boys book series.

I would like to remind you to watch the exclusive Greatest Battles for Boys: The War on Terror video at: bit.ly/3wQWKKC

To find out about upcoming books, join our thriving Facebook Community at: bit.ly/3wQWKKC

If you enjoyed this book, I encourage you to leave a review on the book's page on Amazon.com

Made in the USA
Las Vegas, NV
31 October 2023

79891399R00101